"What I need is a bridegroom and temporary husband."

Cara leaned into Neil, burrowing her cheek against his shoulder. "It wouldn't be a bad deal for a man who liked Italian food," she said with an attempt at humor. "You've eaten my lasagna."

"I sure have, and you're tempting me to volunteer."

"I wish." She kissed him on the cheek and stepped away, gazing at him searchingly. "You wouldn't really consider a pretend marriage, would you, Neil?"

"No, because you're not serious about it," he chided her.

But the look on Cara's face said she was very serious.

And he was seriously tempted!

Dear Reader,

While every romance holds the promise of sweeping readers away with a rugged alpha male or a charismatic cowboy, this month we want to take a closer look at the women who fall in love with our favorite heroes.

"Heroines need to be strong," says Sherryl Woods, author of more than fifty novels. "Readers look for a woman who can stand up to the hero—and stand up to life." Sherryl's book *A Love Beyond Words* features a special heroine who lost her hearing but became stronger because of it. "A heroine needs to triumph over fear or adversity."

Kate Stockwell faces the fear of knowing she cannot bear her own child in Allison Leigh's *Her Unforgettable Fiancé,* the next installment in the STOCKWELLS OF TEXAS miniseries. And an accident forces Josie Scott, Susan Mallery's LONE STAR CANYON heroine in *Wife in Disguise,* to take stock of her life and find a second chance....

In Peggy Webb's *Standing Bear's Surrender,* Sarah Sloan must choose between loyalty and true love! In *Separate Bedrooms...?* by Carole Halston, Cara LaCroix is faced with fulfilling her grandmother's final wish—marriage! And Kirsten Laurence needs the help of the man who broke her heart years ago in Laurie Campbell's *Home at Last.*

"A heroine is a real role model," Sherryl says. And in Special Edition, we aim for every heroine to be a woman we can all admire. Here's to strong women and many more emotionally satisfying reads from Silhouette Special Edition!

Karen Taylor Richman
Senior Editor

Please address questions and book requests to:
Silhouette Reader Service
U.S.: 3010 Walden Ave., P.O. Box 1325, Buffalo, NY 14269
Canadian: P.O. Box 609, Fort Erie, Ont. L2A 5X3

Separate Bedrooms...?

CAROLE HALSTON

Silhouette®

SPECIAL EDITION™

Published by Silhouette Books

America's Publisher of Contemporary Romance

SILHOUETTE BOOKS

ISBN 0-373-24385-5

SEPARATE BEDROOMS...?

Copyright © 2001 by Carole Halston

Visit Silhouette at www.eHarlequin.com

Printed in U.S.A.

Books by Carole Halston

Silhouette Special Edition

Keys to Daniel's House #8
Collision Course #41
The Marriage Bonus #86
Summer Course in Love #115
A Hard Bargain #139
Something Lost,
  Something Gained #163
A Common Heritage #211
The Black Knight #223
Almost Heaven #253
Surprise Offense #291
Matched Pair #328
Honeymoon for One #356
The Baby Trap #388
High Bid #423
Intensive Care #461
Compromising Positions #500
Ben's Touch #543
Unfinished Business #567
Courage To Love #642
Yours, Mine and...Ours #682
The Pride of St. Charles Avenue #800
More Than He Bargained For #829
Bachelor Dad #915
A Self-Made Man #950
The Wrong Man...the Right Time #1089
Mrs. Right #1125
I Take This Man—Again! #1222
Child Most Wanted #1254
Because of the Twins... #1342
Separate Bedrooms...? #1385

Silhouette Romance

Stand-In Bride #62
Love Legacy #83
Undercover Girl #152
Sunset in Paradise #208

Silhouette Books

To Mother with Love 1992
"Neighborly Affair"

CAROLE HALSTON

is a native of south Louisiana, where she lives with her sea-faring husband, Monty, in a rural area on the north shore of Lake Pontchartrain, near New Orleans.

Fans can write Carole at P.O. Box 1095, Madisonville, LA 70447. For a free autographed bookmark, they should send a self-addressed, stamped business-size envelope. Romance readers can visit Carole's Web site by first accessing http://www.eHarlequin.com.

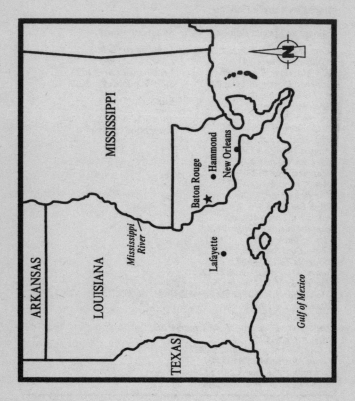

Chapter One

"Who's next, please?" Neil asked as his customer turned to leave with a newly purchased set of brake pads. Half a dozen people were milling about near the long counter of the auto parts store Neil managed and would eventually own after he'd finished buying out his father's interest.

Why hadn't Cara come out of the office to help out? he wondered, looking over his shoulder. It wasn't her job to wait on customers, but Cara was the type of loyal employee who pitched in and did whatever needed to be done without being asked. She knew the whole operation of the business about as well as he did. After all, she'd worked at Griffin Auto Parts either part-time or full-time since she was fifteen, and she'd celebrated her twenty-ninth birthday a couple of months ago.

Through the plate-glass wall, Neil spotted Cara's glossy black curls and frowned, instantly concerned. Seated at her desk and gazing at a computer screen, she was blotting tears from pink cheeks with a tissue. As though sensing his scrutiny, she turned her head and saw him.

Hey, what's wrong? he telegraphed.

She managed a brave smile and waggled her hand, mouthing the words, *I'm okay.*

"I guess I'm next," a woman said, repeating herself with a hint of impatience. Reluctantly Neil returned his attention to his customer, who fished around in her purse for a full minute before she finally pulled out a receipt. "My husband sent me to pick up this part he ordered a couple of days ago. Someone called and said it had come in."

"That was me who called." Cara spoke from beside him, her voice slightly husky. She took the receipt from Neil's hand. "Let me take care of this. You can help someone else who might need some automotive expertise."

"Thanks, Cara," Neil said. He gave her shoulder a gentle squeeze that not only spoke his gratitude, but offered comfort for whatever was troubling her.

It was old habit to feel protective and brotherly to-ward Cara LaCroix, whose name gave clues to her mixed Italian and Cajun French ancestry. He'd known her since she was born. They'd grown up in the same neighborhood right here in Hammond, Louisiana. An only child, Neil was five years older than Cara, the youngest of eight. For some reason, she'd always seemed to idolize him, and he'd thought she was cute as could be with her plump little body, big brown eyes and tangle of black curls.

Neil had picked her up off the sidewalk on any number of occasions when she'd toppled her tricycle. He'd brushed away her tears with awkward tenderness and given her a pep talk. When she'd graduated to a bicycle, he'd done repairs—tightening the chain when it came loose or adjusting the seat. He was enrolled in college by the time she'd become a teenager and begun dating. Instead of turning to her brothers for advice about boys, she'd come to Neil. He'd always listened and tried to be wise.

Before the day was over, Neil figured he would learn what was bothering Cara. He hoped it was nothing serious. If there was a problem he could help solve, well, he wouldn't hesitate to do whatever was in his power to bring a happy smile back to her pretty face. One of his main pleasures in life now was being around Cara and enjoying her full-fledged love of life.

Customers continued to arrive in a steady stream right through the noon hour. Finally about two-thirty, business slacked off to a more normal flow that Neil's two sales clerks, Jimmy Boudreaux and Peewee Oliver, could easily handle.

"You eat lunch yet, Boss?" asked Peewee, an

African-American man in his late twenties whose nickname certainly didn't describe his muscular build.

Cara had just come out of the office. She answered for Neil. "No, he hasn't eaten." She spoke to Neil, "I ordered you a roast beef po'boy earlier. It's in the refrigerator."

"Thanks," Neil said, smiling his appreciation. "That was sweet of you."

"Somebody has to see that you don't go hungry now that your mom and dad have moved away to Florida. I'll bet you skip at least one meal a day," she chided him.

Neil couldn't honestly deny her accusation. If eating wasn't convenient, he could easily skip a meal. He'd regained some enjoyment of food during the last three years since he'd lost his wife and small son and his whole world had disintegrated, but food would never taste as good as it had when he'd been a happily married man with a family. None of life's rewards would ever be the same again. That was something he accepted.

At least the terrible grief had softened with time into sadness. The key to surviving tragedy, he'd discovered, was keeping busy and not thinking a lot about himself.

"Hey, skipping a few meals doesn't hurt me," he declared, gesturing toward his tall, lanky frame. "It's my diet plan."

Cara made a batting motion with her hand. "Diet plan. You could eat a million calories a day and not gain a pound. All I have to do is take one bite of a rich dessert and the scales jump five pounds.''

''You worry too much about your weight.''

''If I don't, I'll end up wearing the same large sizes as my three sisters.''

''Their husbands don't complain, do they?'' Neil draped his arm around her shoulders and gave her a brotherly hug. ''Come and share my po'boy. You probably had a salad for lunch that didn't even satisfy your hunger pains.''

She sighed, walking along with him toward the small room that served as an employees' lounge. ''I did. And I'm starving. The salad had that nasty non-fat so-called Italian dressing on it.'' She shuddered. ''No self-respecting Italian that I know would make a dressing without real olive oil.''

Neil grinned at her expressiveness.

At the door of the lounge, Cara came to a standstill. ''I'd better get back to work.''

''Take a break and keep me company,'' Neil urged. ''We haven't had a chance to chat today.'' He hadn't forgotten that she'd been crying earlier, and he was still concerned about the reason.

''Okay, but I can't promise I'll be very cheerful,'' she said, relenting.

''Why not? Are you feeling depressed about your grandmother's health?''

Cara nodded, blinking hard to hold back tears that suddenly welled up in her eyes. Neil gently drew her inside the lounge and pulled out a chair at the table while he lectured in a sympathetic tone, "We've already talked about this. Sophia is a very religious woman. She's not afraid of death. She's even looking forward to being reunited with deceased loved ones in Heaven."

"I know all that."

Cara resisted letting him seat her. "You sit down," she said. "I'll get your po'boy for you. What would you like to drink?"

"I can wait on myself. You don't need to serve me."

"I don't mind."

"Sit."

Neil was already on his way to the refrigerator. He was more interested in getting to the bottom of her unhappiness than he was in having his lunch, but he figured he might as well humor her. After retrieving the sandwich loaf, he unwrapped it on the counter and used a kitchen knife to cut each half loaf into quarters. Then he transferred the po'boy over to the table, the white butcher paper doubling as a plate. Before he sat down across from Cara, he got each of them a canned drink from the refrigerator, a diet cola for her and an iced tea for himself.

"Help yourself," he offered and bit into crusty French bread.

"I shouldn't."

"Sure tastes good. If you take the edge off your appetite, you can eat a light supper."

"That's true. And, darn it, I'm starving." She

picked up a sandwich section and began to eat it, obviously relishing the taste of roast beef and provolone cheese. Still, her expression remained downcast, Neil noticed with compassion.

"Back to our conversation about Sophia," he said when she'd dusted the crumbs off her fingers and sat back. Going on past experience, he knew that pouring out her thoughts and feelings to him would be therapeutic. "Is she going downhill faster than the doctor told the family she would?" Several months ago, the oncologist in charge of Sophia's care had given a life-expectancy range of eight months to a year. Sophia had opted not to subject herself to chemotherapy when she was diagnosed with lymphoma.

"No." Cara's voice broke, and tears spilled down her cheeks. She wiped them away impatiently.

"Something happened since yesterday. Tell me about it. Maybe I can help."

"You can't help." She sniffled and pointed a forefinger toward the uneaten half of his po'boy as a reminder that he should keep eating. Neil dutifully picked up another sandwich quarter to pacify her. Cara filled him in without any more prodding. "This morning I stopped off at my parents' house on the way here to spend a few minutes with Nonna, like I do several mornings a week." Neil nodded, familiar with her routine. He didn't need her to explain that *nonna* was Italian for grandmother.

Cara went on, "I let myself in through the back door and went straight to Nonna's bedroom, figuring

I'd poke my head in the kitchen and say hi to Mamma on my way out. The door to Nonna's bedroom was open and I heard Mamma's voice and Nonna's voice. I didn't mean to eavesdrop, but before I could call out, I started listening to their conversation. Nonna was telling Mamma that she'd dreamed I'd gotten married. She described my wedding gown and the dresses my attendants wore. She described the flowers in the church. Neil, you should have heard Nonna's voice. She sounded so happy, recalling every detail of her dream.'' Cara bit into her quivering bottom lip and wiped away two more huge tears.

"Go on," he prompted gently, getting the picture now, but wanting to let her finish out her explanation.

"Then she and my mom talked about the fact that I'm twenty-nine years old and not even engaged to be married. Nonna said if only her dream had been real, she could die without a single regret. Her main reason for trying to hang on was wishing she could see me settled down with a good husband."

"You poor kid. What a guilt trip." Neil's warm sympathy was mixed with exasperation. "That family of yours mean well, but they've been putting pressure on you to find a husband since you were twenty years old."

"It's because they all love me. They can't conceive of anyone, man or woman, staying single and being really fulfilled and content." Cara sighed, slumping forward and resting folded arms on the table. "I agree with them. That's the hard part. I'd give anything to be planning a wedding for Nonna to attend while she's still strong enough. Not just for her sake but because I'd like nothing better than to be getting married. I always planned to be a wife and mother, but it just hasn't *happened.*''

"The right guy will come along. You have to be patient." Neil had pushed aside the remains of his lunch. He reached over and clasped her forearms, giving them a reassuring squeeze.

"I've been patient! What if I keep waiting for Mr. Right and he doesn't come along? What if he's already come and gone, and I didn't recognize him? Neil, how will I *know* a certain guy is the one?"

"Your instincts will tell you he's the one. When you imagine living the rest of your life without him, you won't be able to stand the thought."

"Is that the way you felt when you proposed to Lisa?"

"Yes." Neil quickly shoved the memory back behind a closed door of his past, but not before he'd been flooded with painful remembrance.

"I'm sorry." Cara took one of his hands between hers, their roles quickly reversed with her offering him support. "That question just slipped out. I know you can't bear reminiscing because you're still grieving over Lisa and little Chris."

"I'm okay," Neil assured her. He stood up. "Don't brood over what you overheard this morning, Cara. I'm sure you're doing a lot to make Sophia's remaining time on earth happy, just by being yourself."

She sat there instead of rising to her feet. Neil looked at her questioningly.

"Do you have another minute?" she asked. "There's more."

He waited for her to elaborate, suddenly uneasy for reasons he didn't quite fathom.

"Last night Roy asked me to marry him."

Neil slowly sat back down. Roy Xavier was the automobile salesman she'd been dating for quite a while, but Neil hadn't gotten the impression she was serious about the guy. "What was your answer?"

"I sort of turned him down."

" 'Sort of'?"

"I told him the truth. That I like him and enjoy his company on our dates, but I don't think I'm in love with him." She studied Neil's face closely, an anxious frown cutting tiny lines between her eyebrows. "You seem relieved I didn't say yes."

"Your announcement took me by surprise," he said, not comfortable with admitting that he *was* relieved. Neil didn't understand himself why his gut reaction to the idea of her marrying Roy Xavier had been so strongly negative, other than the fact that nobody she'd ever dated had seemed good enough for her.

"I wasn't prepared for him to propose," she confided. "I stammered around, like an idiot. Thoughts were whirling around in my head. I didn't want to hurt his feelings, plus a part of my brain was ticking off Roy's qualifications that would make him a good husband for me.'' She used her fingers now to tick off those qualifications as she listed them for Neil. ''He's a good-hearted guy. He's successful at his job. Most months he's the top car salesman at the dealership. He's a church going man. He's from a large family. I haven't been around his parents a lot, but I like them just fine, and he seems to like mine.'' In her expressive way, Cara threw up her hands. ''Why *not* marry Roy? That's the question. Especially when I'll be thirty years old my next birthday.''

''You said yourself you're not in love with him. Not after dating him for what, six months?''

''Six and a half months actually.'' She resumed her argument with Neil and with herself. ''Maybe there are some people in the world who don't ever fall head over heels in love. Maybe with those people, love grows gradually out of respect and affection. Romantic love doesn't last anyway, right?''

''Cara, you're trying to talk yourself into marrying Roy Xavier.''

''You think I'd be making a big mistake?''

Yes. Neil clamped his jaw closed to keep from speaking the definite reply that rose to his lips. ''What I think doesn't matter. It's your life and your decision. But don't feel pressured into marrying Roy or anybody else just because you're tired of being single and would like to make your grandmother happy.''

''But you don't dislike Roy?''

''I don't know Roy well enough to like or dislike

him. He seems like a nice enough guy,'' Neil added, aware that he sounded grudging.

Cara held out her left hand and gazed wistfully at her bare ring finger. ''He didn't buy an engagement ring. He said we could go shopping together and pick one out.''

''So Roy hasn't given up hope that you'll say yes, I take it.''

''Oh, no. He was disappointed by my reaction to his proposal, naturally, but he's willing to give me some time.'' She placed her palms on the table and levered herself up. ''Thanks, Neil, for listening to another segment in the Life of Cara soap opera. I feel better now, more able to cope. Talking to you about a problem always has that effect on me.''

Neil didn't feel good at all about the outcome of the heart-to-heart talk they'd had. In fact, suddenly his mood was lousy.

''Boss, a sales rep is out here and wants to talk to you.'' Peewee stuck his head in the doorway to speak to Neil. He named the muffler company the sales person was representing.

''Tell him I'll be right out,'' Neil said.

''Will do.'' Peewee left.

Cara came around the table. ''You go and talk to the rep. I'll tidy up,'' she said.

''You're not the maid around here.''

Neil had made that point clear in an employees' meeting recently. He'd posted a new sign, restating his father's old rule that each person using the lounge was to clean up after himself or herself out of consideration for fellow employees. Cara hadn't complained to Neil, but he'd noticed that she was taking it upon herself to clear the table and tidy up when her co-workers didn't bother to pick up after themselves.

"Don't be so doggoned self-sufficient," she scolded him, slapping his hand lightly away as he reached for his empty beverage can. "I like to do something nice for you when I get the chance. It's payback time." Cara stood on tiptoe and kissed him on the cheek, then gave him a shove toward the door.

"Thanks, Cara."

"You're welcome."

With efficient movements, she crumpled up the butcher paper around the uneaten portion of the po'boy. He'd gotten down most of his three-quarters of the sandwich, much to Cara's satisfaction. Now if he didn't eat a square meal for supper, at least he'd had some nourishment today, she reflected.

Cara only wished she could do more than help Neil run his business and make sure that he ate right. She worried about him and her heart ached for him when she thought about all that he'd been through, losing his wife and child. They'd been killed in a terrible ten-automobile pile-up on a Memphis interstate. Lisa and three-year-old Chris, along with a dozen other people, had simply been unlucky enough to be on the highway at the wrong time.

Neil had been out of town, doing his job as a sales

rep for a major manufacturer of automobile parts. Cara sensed that in low moments he might sometimes wish he'd perished with his family instead of having been spared their fate. But she thanked God for sparing him. She loved Neil every bit as much as she loved her four brothers, and, truth be told, she was closer to him than to Tony or Michael or Sal or Frankie.

Cara had been raised with the philosophy that everything happens for a reason, and all events figure into a divine plan that humans may not comprehend. It was impossible to understand why a wonderful guy like Neil would have such a horrible thing happen to him, but Cara couldn't help but be glad for herself that he'd come back into her life three years ago when he quit his job and moved back here from Memphis, a thirty one-year-old widower.

Every day when she came to work she looked forward to seeing Neil. What was it he'd told her today about knowing when Mr. Right came along? An empty can in either hand, Cara paused on her way over to the recyclables bin, recalling Neil's exact words: *When you imagine living the rest of your life without him, you won't be able to stand the thought.*

What she couldn't imagine was ever wanting to work at a different job with another boss besides Neil. Whether or not she married Roy, Cara would keep her job. She would continue to see Neil every day. Their relationship wouldn't change.

With the lounge restored to a spic-and-span state, Cara returned to the office and tackled her work with renewed energy. Somehow her ruminations about her stable job situation had eased a great deal of the anxiety of deciding whether to accept or reject Roy Xavier's marriage proposal.

Chapter Two

"Thank you, Aunt Cara!" chorused four-year-old Lea and Lauren in unison. They'd just ripped open Cara's birthday gifts, identical little-girl makeup kits. "Now we can put on makeup and look pretty, like you!"

Mia, the twins' mother, feigned insult, arms akimbo. "Your mommy puts on makeup once in a while and looks pretty, too, when she has time."

"It doesn't do your Aunt Cara a lot of good to primp," Cara's oldest brother Tony addressed his young nieces, a wide grin on his face.

"Oh, no, here we go again," groaned Cara, clapping her hands over her ears.

Tony raised his voice. "Because Aunt Cara can't seem to catch her a man to marry."

"Stop picking on your baby sister," scolded Rose LaCroix, eyeing her eldest son fondly.

The twins were more interested in their pile of presents than in adult verbal exchanges. They tore the wrappings from two more packages and drew general attention back to themselves, but Cara knew it was only a matter of time before she came in for more half teasing, half serious ribbing about her single status. She'd almost come to dread large family gatherings like this one.

Today the crowd on her parents' rear lawn included all eight LaCroix siblings, the wives and husbands of the seven who were happily married, twenty-five grandchildren and assorted neighbors and relatives. Cara hadn't counted heads, but there were between fifty-five and sixty people present. The youngest was her brother Sal's six-month-old baby boy, Stevie, who was being passed around and tossed in the air and played with. The oldest was Sophia, holding court in a lawn chair and looking frail in a new ruffled pink duster.

Cara had helped her grandmother get dressed earlier. She'd combed Sophia's fine silver hair, dusted face power and a touch of blush on her dear old wrinkled, gaunt cheeks, and fastened her antique garnet earrings in her ears. While she'd chattered on about various subjects, Cara kept remembering the conversation she'd overheard yesterday morning when her grandmother had described her wonderful dream about attending Cara's wedding. Cara had imagined Sophia's thrilled reaction if her youngest—and favorite—granddaughter confided, "Nonna, guess what? The man I'm dating, Roy Xavier? He proposed, and I've decided to say yes!"

Cara *had* almost decided. She'd gone over and over the pros and cons of marrying Roy and come up with all pros except for one single con—she wasn't crazy in love with him. But maybe she never *would* fall crazily in love. A year or two from now, Cara might look back and regret turning Roy down.

The *only* thing holding Cara back at this point was Neil's opposition. She'd always valued his advice and sought his approval.

Neil was the only person in her circle of important people Cara could trust to be discreet. That was why she hadn't confided in any of her three sisters or her mother or Sophia. Rose would tell Sophia, swearing her to secrecy, and vice versa. They would tell Natalie, Cara's oldest sister, once again admonishing her not to tell a soul. Natalie would pass along the news to Angie in strictest confidence. Angie would tell Mia. Inevitably the three sisters' husbands would be made privy to the secret and they'd tell Cara's brothers, who would tell their wives. It would be just a matter of time before Cara's personal business would become *the* hot topic of family discussion. Everybody would have an opinion and state it— To one another and to Cara, who had learned the hard way not to be a blabber-mouth about her private life.

"We love *all* our presents!" sang out Lea and Lauren once all the packages had been opened, responding prettily to coaching from their mother.

"Now can we play Pin the Tail on the Donkey?" asked one of the twins' cousins, setting off a litany of childish requests to play the traditional LaCroix birthday party game.

Eighteen-year-old Mark, the oldest LaCroix grandchild, good-naturedly carried out his assignment for the afternoon, herding the crowd of children over to an outside wall of the garage. A large poster of a donkey, much repaired with transparent tape had already been thumbtacked to the white-painted boards.

"There's more cake and ice cream for seconds," Rose informed the adults over the din of laughter and a dozen different conversations.

Cara was just now taking her turn at holding six-month-old Stevie. "Aren't you precious?" she cooed to her little nephew as he gurgled and smiled at her.

"Hey, could Carmen and I have everybody's attention? We have some big news to share." The request came from Cara's youngest brother Frankie, who at thirty was only a year and some months older than her. Heads turned in his direction. Frankie hugged his wife close to his side, and the two of them grinned at each other, like co-conspirators. "Looks like Stevie's gonna have a little cousin playmate in less than nine months. Carmen's expecting again."

Cara added her sincere congratulations to the cacophony and tried not to look wistful. She and Carmen had been classmates in school, and now the other woman was pregnant for the third time and obviously blissfully happy about her condition.

For a few seconds Cara fantasized, visualizing Roy and herself here in the midst of the LaCroix family, making a similar announcement. Roy would look every bit as proud as Frankie did. Cara could feel his arm around her, strong and supportive.

The fantasy could easily come true. All Cara had to do was tell Roy she'd made up her mind and wanted to marry him. Immediately she could set a date for just a few months from now and start making whirl-wind wedding plans to insure that Sophia was well enough to attend. How Cara wanted her grandmother to be there when she walked down the aisle, finally a bride instead of a bridesmaid.

It would make Sophia so happy. It would make the whole family happy and would mark the end to Cara's being the lone unmarried sibling.

Stevie had begun to fret. His mother, Barb, appeared and reached for him, saying, "I'll bet my little guy is hungry." Feeding Stevie was strictly his mom's job, since Barb was breast-feeding. Cara handed the infant over reluctantly. Her arms felt empty. She felt absurdly alone, an *oddity,* in the midst of her large, affectionate family.

I want to be half of a married couple, she thought. I want to get pregnant and have a baby. I want to be a wife, a mommy, a married daughter and granddaughter and sister.

She could have what she so badly wanted.

I'll do it, Cara promised herself silently. She sucked in a breath of deep relief as the vapor of indecision evaporated. In its place grew an urgency to talk to Roy as soon as possible. She would tell him right away, before she even said hello. Yes, yes, yes, I will marry you.

Cara didn't want to waste a minute getting things in motion now that her mind was made up.

"That's really eye-catching," Cara said. She'd walked up behind Neil. He was near the front of the store setting up a display of car waxes and polishes. "Is that a new product? The bright blue can?"

"Yes, it's supposed to be the hottest new car wax on the market."

"Really. I'll have to tell Roy. He keeps that car of his so shiny you can see your reflection in it."

"Yes, he does keep it waxed to a high shine. But then cars are his business." Neil managed to keep his voice even, not an easy feat when he was talking about Cara's husband-to-be. The more he was around Roy Xavier, the more Neil disliked the man.

And since Cara had gotten engaged to Xavier two weeks ago, the car salesman had taken to dropping by the store often. Neil's gut instinct told him that, despite a phony show of friendliness, Xavier didn't like him, either.

"Roy is coming by to pick me up. We're meeting with Father Kerby at the church." Cara had tipped her head back and hunched up her shoulders.

"What's wrong? Tense muscles?" Neil asked.

"Planning this wedding is killing me," she declared, rolling her head in a circle. "I try not to get uptight, but there's so much to be done in such a short time."

"You're pushing yourself too hard. Here. Let me work out some of the knots for you." Neil turned her so that she faced away from him. Then he began to massage her neck and shoulders.

"That feels *so* good," she said. "I need you to do this before I go to bed at night. Then maybe I could fall asleep right away."

Roy Xavier spoke from behind Neil. "Hey, I object. The only man who's giving my woman a massage at bedtime from now on is me."

"Oh, hi, Roy," Cara said, her voice lazy with relaxation. "Just give me another minute or two of this heaven."

"We're kind of short on time, baby," he replied.

"Are we? Too bad. Thanks, Neil." With a sigh, she pulled away reluctantly, and Neil dropped his hands just as reluctantly.

"How are things going, Roy?" he asked, striving to sound genial. Hearing Xavier address Cara as *baby* in a tone of ownership had grated on Neil's nerves.

"Couldn't be better," the other man replied. His clipped tone jarred with his usual smooth salesman's manner.

Cara didn't seem to notice anything amiss. "I'll be about thirty minutes late tomorrow morning, Neil. I have to run by the printer's on my way to work and look at some sample wedding invitations.''

''Take your time,'' he said. ''You need to slow down a little. You're running yourself ragged getting your wedding organized.''

''Ready, baby?'' Xavier drew Cara close and kissed her on the mouth. He would have turned it into a lingering kiss if Cara had cooperated, but she didn't, Neil noticed, his fists clenching with repugnance.

''I just need to get my handbag. Bye, Neil.''

''See you tomorrow.'' Neil averted his head, fixing his gaze on the display instead of watching them leave together, Xavier's arm around Cara's waist, staking possession.

The guy wasn't nearly good enough for Cara. Why couldn't she see what a mistake she was making? She was just settling for Roy Xavier because she was ready to marry *some*body, but mainly because she so badly wanted to make her grandmother happy. Neil was convinced that the business about Sophia's dream had tipped the scales for Cara.

He didn't know how he was going to force himself to attend the wedding. Just the thought of watching the ceremony made Neil want to *do* something to intercede.

Cara was making a mistake. She wasn't going to be happy as Roy Xavier's wife. No way.

''Roy, it's fine to give me a peck on the lips to say hello in front of Neil, but I wish you wouldn't kiss me as though we had privacy,'' Cara said after she and Roy had left the store. ''It embarrasses me and makes Neil uncomfortable.'' Her cheeks still felt flushed with her annoyance.

''He looked way too comfortable putting his hands all over you,'' Roy replied, his voice angry.

''Don't be ridiculous! He didn't have his 'hands all over me'! He was massaging my neck and shoulders. Neil has *never* touched me in any sexual way.''

''Every time I come into the store, he's hugging you or patting you. I don't like it one bit.''

''That's an exaggeration. Even if it were true, Neil and I are like brother and sister.''

Roy grunted skeptically.

They got into his car. Cara wanted to say more, but she decided to let the subject drop for now. Before she could start up a friendlier exchange, Roy spoke in a more conciliatory tone.

''Let's don't fight, baby. But try to see things from my point of point. How would you like walking into the dealership and seeing me being familiar with one of the secretaries?''

''I wouldn't like it. But you haven't had a lifelong friendship with one of them, have you?''

Roy held up his hand, and Cara interpreted the gesture as signaling the end of the discussion. She stayed silent while he pulled out onto the street, deciding to let him start up a different conversation.

''Griffin was right about one thing.'' Roy took his right hand off the wheel and rested it on her thigh.

"You *are* running yourself ragged organizing our wedding and working a full-time job. I say go ahead and quit the job now. Give him two weeks' notice, of course."

"Quit my job?" Cara was staring at him in utter surprise.

"We both want to start a family right away, right? Didn't we agree on that?" He rubbed her thigh suggestively. "At the risk of bragging, I expect to make you pregnant during our honeymoon."

"I never said anything about quitting my job when I got pregnant. I'm sure Neil will give me maternity leave the last month or two, if I need to take leave."

"You'll have plenty to do to keep you busy without working. Things like decorating a nursery for the baby. Plus keeping house and cooking meals. Remember, I warned you I'm an old-fashioned kind of guy who likes the idea of being the breadwinner."

"You warned me you like being the *main* breadwinnner, which is okay with me. But I don't think I would like being totally dependent. You have to realize I've worked and earned my own spending money since I was fifteen."

"Then get another job. Dammit, I don't want you working for Griffin." He took his hand away from Cara's thigh, just moments before she shoved it away.

"I can't *believe* you're jealous of Neil! That's so *ridiculous!*"

"The guy's against you marrying me, Cara. I can tell."

Cara opened her mouth to object and then pressed her lips closed when she realized she couldn't honestly speak a denial. Roy looked over at her knowingly. "I'll bet he tried to talk you out of accepting my marriage proposal, didn't he?"

"Whatever kind of advice Neil gave me prior to our becoming engaged, his only concern was my happiness. Ever since I told him I was going to marry you, he hasn't said the first negative word. And he would *never* do or say anything to undermine our marriage once we're husband and wife. Neil's too honorable a person."

"He's got you convinced he's some kind of saint. That's for certain," Roy muttered.

"Darn it, I wanted the two of you to be good friends."

"Fat chance."

Cara sighed, her anger ebbing and leaving her deflated. "This puts a damper on everything, Roy. My job is a big part of my identity, just like your job is a big part of who you are."

"But you're going to change your identity and become my wife, Cara. You're going to become the mother of our kids."

"And you're going to become my husband and the father of our kids."

He sucked in a breath and expelled it noisily. "Cara, you're not telling me you'd back out of marrying me before you'd quit working for Griffin?"

"I'm saying it's unreasonable for you to expect me to quit a job I love."

The quarrel continued until they arrived at the church. Cara was so upset that she could barely concentrate on anything Father Kerby said during the premarital counseling session.

Afterwards Roy made a stiff offer to take her out to supper, and Cara refused, asking him to drive her back to the store where she'd left her car. He complied, obviously still furious at her.

Neil's garage doors were raised. Cara glimpsed him bent over beneath the raised hood of the old car he was restoring, a 1954 Corvette. Following the same instinct that had led her to his house, she pulled into the driveway and got out.

He straightened up, wiping his hands on a rag as she approached. Country and western music played on a portable boom box sitting on a shelf. Cara was reminded of the many times she'd gone looking for him at different stages in her life, when she was down in the dumps about something and needed to talk. Often she'd found him tinkering with his car in his parents' garage.

"Hi, there," Neil greeted her now. His tone was gentle and his gaze perceptive. It wasn't necessary to tell him she felt lousy. He was reading that message in her face and body language, she knew.

"Hi. Just like the old days, huh? Except your taste

in music has changed. You used to listen to rock and roll.''

He shrugged. ''Occasionally I tune in a classic rock station.''

''Too many painful memories?'' Cara's voice was soft with sympathy as she filled in the gaps of what he hadn't needed to explain. Some of those hit songs on classic rock stations would take him back to the era when he'd dated Lisa, back to their married years.

''Yes. You and Roy had a spat?'' he asked. As always, he seemed more interested in her than himself.

''It was more than a spat. Neil, he insists I quit my job!'' she burst out.

''I was afraid of that.''

''He's actually *jealous* of you! I tried to tell him that you're like a brother to me, but I couldn't seem to get it through that thick skull of his that my relationship with you poses no threat to him.''

Neil crossed his arms and leaned against the car. The slump of his shoulders spelled out resignation. ''It won't be easy to replace you, but I certainly understand your position.''

''My position is that I'm *not* quitting.''

He sighed, rubbing a hand down the back of his head and neck. ''Cara, there's a lot of give and take in a marriage.''

''Roy's being unreasonable. He's not considering my feelings. I love my job. When I said yes to him, it was with the full intention of continuing working. For years and years.''

"You plan to have a family, don't you?"

Cara bobbed her head in the affirmative. "Yes, but so what? I figured you wouldn't mind if I set up a playpen at the store like Allison did when she had Jessica." Allison was one of the two other women employees who worked in the office under Cara's supervision. "Remember how we all pitched in and helped take care of Jessica? Even Jimmy and Pee-wee?"

"Maybe Roy will come around."

"He'd better." Cara stood on tiptoes and kissed him on the cheek, letting her actions thank him for listening and being there for her, centering her world. He responded in kind, silently saying You're welcome with a brief, warm hug. "See you tomorrow," she called over her shoulder as she walked to her car.

"Drive carefully," he called back, his tone sober and concerned.

On the way to her apartment, Cara remembered the question Roy had asked her this afternoon during their heated argument: *You're not telling me you'd back out of marrying me before you'd quit working for Griffin?*

Yes, Roy, that's what I'm telling you, she thought now. She simply couldn't marry anyone who expected her to cut Neil out of her life. For that was what Roy actually demanded.

Even though Neil had never said as much, Cara knew intuitively that he needed her to be there for him, too. She brightened up his day-to-day existence. Under no circumstances was she going to abandon him.

If Roy couldn't understand, then he definitely wasn't the right husband for Cara. She needed to call a halt to the wedding plans.

Her whole family would be terribly disappointed, but no more disappointed than Cara would at postponing becoming a married woman. By the time she eventually did find a better husband prospect—a man more considerate of her needs—Sophia would have passed away. Cara would live the rest of her days regretting that she hadn't fulfilled her grandmother's wish to attend her favorite granddaughter's wedding.

Moving like an old man, Neil closed the garage doors after Cara's car had disappeared from sight. Her visit had robbed him of all incentive to resume his repairs to the engine of the car. After turning off the boom box, he went inside his silent house.

For all her bravado, Neil expected that Cara would give in to Xavier's ultimatum that she quit her job at Griffin's Auto Parts. What choice did she have?— other than to cancel the wedding, and she wouldn't go that far. Those same pressures that had caused her to settle for Xavier were still operative, primary among them the desire to grant her dying grandmother's fervent wish to see Cara married.

In a matter of a few weeks or a couple of months at most, Cara would no longer be Neil's employee. He wouldn't have daily contact with her. For a while she'd keep in touch, dropping by the store occasionally or calling him on the phone. Then she'd get caught up in her world that didn't include him any more.

The whole chain of events he foresaw was so damned depressing. And yet Neil couldn't let Cara suspect how her absence from his life would affect him. Not for anything would he cause her guilt on his behalf.

Xavier might as well snatch the sun right out of the sky as deprive Neil of Cara's sunny presence.

In the kitchen, Neil opened the refrigerator and closed it. He wasn't hungry, and the effort to fix himself even the simplest meal didn't seem worth the trouble.

Chapter Three

Cara stuck her head in the door of the stockroom, where Neil was training a new stockboy. "Neil, I'm going to the post office now. Can I run any errands for you while I'm out and about?"

"Hmm, seems like there was some errand," he replied, scratching his head. "I'll walk out with you. Maybe it'll come to me." Mainly Neil was seizing the opportunity to talk to Cara one-on-one.

Three days had gone by since she'd come to his house. She'd been awfully subdued for someone usually so outgoing and carefree. He hadn't questioned her about the status of her relationship with Xavier out of respect for her privacy, instead waiting for her to come to him. But so far she hadn't, and Neil was concerned about her.

"Is everything okay?" he asked when they'd emerged from the store, both of them pausing to carry on conversation. "Did you patch things up with Xavier?"

Cara sighed. "Yes, but it's not going to work out. I've decided to break up with him."

"I noticed he hasn't been around."

"He's making a big deal about not coming here to the store in order to avoid you. But there are more issues than my job. Roy's turned out to be a domineering type. I would never be happy married to him." She mustered a smile. "Your instincts were right on target, not surprisingly."

"Better to find out now," he said, his voice gruff with sympathy.

"If only I hadn't talked myself into saying yes to him. You don't know how I dread breaking the news to my family that there isn't going to be a wedding. I'll never live this down." She closed her eyes and shuddered. "What a mess. Nonna and my mother and sisters didn't waste a minute going shopping for their outfits to wear. They all spent a fortune."

"They haven't worn the outfits. Can't they be returned?"

"That's not the point. It's just going to be such a big letdown for the whole family." Cara shook her head slowly, her pretty face haunted. "Especially Nonna. It was so cruel of me to give her a false sense of happiness. Last night I lay awake half the night, trying to think of some solution. I even considered begging Roy to go through with the wedding with the agreement that we'd only stay married while Nonna was alive. Then we'd get a divorce. But I know he wouldn't do it.''

''That's a crazy idea. You poor kid. I wish there was something I could do to help you out.'' Neil wrapped his arms around her and hugged her close, not really caring that cars were passing by on the street behind the store parking lot.

Cara leaned into him, burrowing her cheek against his shoulder. ''What I need is a bridegroom and temporary husband. It wouldn't be a bad deal for a man who liked Italian food,'' she said with a brave attempt at humor. ''You've eaten my lasagne.''

''I sure have, and you're tempting me to volunteer.''

''I wish.'' She kissed him on the cheek and stepped away, glancing out toward the street. ''There goes Agnes Tanner in that green car, talking on her trusty cell phone. The whole town will be abuzz with her description of us in a clench outside the store.''

''Then our romance following your breakup up with Xavier won't come as any great surprise,'' Neil said lightly, wanting to make her smile at his ridiculous statement.

Cara gazed at him searchingly. ''You wouldn't *really* consider a fake romance, would you, Neil?''

''No, because you're not serious about a fake marriage,'' he chided her.

''I could be serious if you were willing. It wouldn't

be at all unpleasant sharing a house with you for six months or a year. We get along great. You wouldn't invade my space and I wouldn't invade yours. But, I realize that would be asking far too much.'' She turned to leave and then stopped. ''Was there an errand?''

''Yes, but I still don't remember what it was.'' He waved her on and went back inside, no less worried about her well-being than he'd been before she'd filled him in. She'd gotten herself into a no-win situation with the best of intentions. Neil was afraid she would cave in to all the pressures bearing on her and end up going through with marrying Xavier rather than cancel the wedding and disappoint her family.

Damn it, he wouldn't stand by and let her do something that desperate. If nothing else, he would agree to participate in her far-fetched scheme to fake a marriage.

Why not? He wasn't dating anyone, didn't foresee wanting to date anyone, ever. Cara was wrong. It wouldn't be asking too much of him. Not too much at all.

The talk with Neil hadn't erased Cara's dilemma, but, as always, she felt better after confiding in him, more positive that things would be okay. Somehow. Some way.

It surprised—and intrigued—her that he hadn't been more emphatic in his refusal when she'd asked, *You wouldn't really consider a fake romance?*

Cara couldn't help wondering whether she could actually persuade Neil to agree to a temporary marriage. Whether or not he would go that far to help her out, she would never know because she wouldn't ask that big a favor of him.

And yet...

The idea *was* crazy. Not to mention the dishonesty involved in speaking marriage vows with the intention of not staying married. But wouldn't the good outweigh the bad? Wouldn't God understand? How could it be wrong to grant Nonna's wish to attend Cara's wedding before she died?

However, Cara wouldn't have to wrestle with the morality of a temporary marriage. She wouldn't bring the subject up again with Neil, and he was her only candidate for a temporary husband.

Cara couldn't imagine entering into such an arrangement and living for a period of time with any other man she knew. Not even Roy. Odd how easily she *could* imagine moving into Neil's house and becoming his housemate.

The imaginary scenario occupied her mind while she drove to and from the post office. On her return to the store, she gave herself a stern lecture. *It's not going to happen, Cara, so let's get back on track and focus on reality. Okay?*

"Okay," she said aloud glumly.

True to her word, she put aside the whole train of thought, though unwillingly.

"Cara, if you're not in a big hurry, could you stick around a few minutes?" Neil asked.

"Sure."

It was quitting time, and the store employees were leaving. Cara did a few tasks and straightened her desk, not finding Neil's request unusual. She assumed he wanted to discuss some store-related matter.

As soon as everyone had gone, he came back into the office. "Are you seeing Xavier tonight?" he inquired.

"No, he has a poker game."

Her answer seemed to give him pause. "Then why don't I take you out to dinner?"

Cara's immediate reaction was pleasure. "I'd like that."

"Good. I'll pick you up about seven o'clock."

"Where are we going? Just so I'll know how to dress."

He named a popular restaurant that served steak and seafood.

On the way to her apartment Cara wondered what had prompted Neil to issue the invitation. Did she look so down in the dumps that he'd felt sorry for her? Whatever the reason, she was glad. It would be a treat to get together with Neil away from the store. Cara meant to keep the conversation on subjects other than her problems.

As she changed clothes and freshened her makeup, Cara found herself remembering how as a preteen girl she'd daydreamed about getting old enough to date Neil. She'd been so envious of his girlfriends. Cara was seventeen and going steady with her current heartthrob when Neil became engaged to be married, but she still suffered jealous pangs when she met Lisa, Neil's fiancée and later his wife.

If tonight were really a date, it would be the realization of a lot of wishful thinking at more youthful stages of Cara's life. But tonight wasn't really a date. Cara and Neil were long-time friends, employee and employer. He wasn't—and never would be—interested in her as a woman. The grown-up Cara accepted that fact of life and was happy with their relationship.

But what if Neil *were* interested in her? Cara brushed aside the question, since such speculation was pointless.

Neil arrived a couple of minutes early. Cara was ready and keeping a watch out for him. He'd changed clothes, too, she noticed as she climbed into the passenger seat of his pickup. Instead of his khaki pants and red knit shirt with his first name and Griffin Auto Parts embroidered on the pocket, he was wearing navy slacks and a crisp striped shirt. He looked clean-cut and handsome, his sandy hair neatly combed and his tanned skin emphasizing the blue of his eyes.

It occurred to Cara as she clipped her seatbelt, that Neil's looks appealed to her a whole lot more than Roy's ever had. The honest insight made her feel guilty. Talking herself into marrying Roy just because he was available and willing hadn't been fair to him.

"Mom said to tell you hello," Neil said. "She called right after I got home from the store."

"How is her golf game coming along?"

"Not too good. But she's having fun playing with a group of retirees who're also beginners."

"Is your dad managing to keep himself occupied?"

"Yes, he's discovered the Internet and is looking up old army buddies."

"How neat."

They chatted about his parents on the short drive to the restaurant. Cara's interest was genuine; she was very fond of Dean and Judith Griffin and had missed them since they'd moved off to Florida.

"Maybe I should have gotten a reservation," Neil said, parking his pickup in one of the few available spots. "I didn't think it would be this crowded on a weeknight."

Inside they were able to get a table. Not surprisingly, Cara recognized a number of friends and acquaintances, as did Neil. They responded to greetings, following behind the hostess.

"I thought that was Agnes Tanner's car outside," Cara commented when they were seated. "Wouldn't you know she would pick this same restaurant tonight?"

"So what?" he replied.

"She just happens to be the biggest gossip in Hammond. You know that."

Neil grinned. "Should we give her something juicy to gossip about?"

Cara hadn't seen that streak of playfulness in Neil during the three years since he'd returned to his home town a widower. "Let's," she replied, smiling impishly.

He leaned across the table, picked up one of Cara's hands and brought it to his mouth and kissed her knuckles. Cara felt a jolt of electricity at the contact of his lips against her skin. Warm pleasure gushed through her, all the way to her toes. Wow, she almost said before she caught herself.

"Was she watching?" he asked, returning her hand to the table.

Cara had forgotten all about Agnes Tanner. She glanced in the woman's direction. "*Gawking* is more the word."

Apparently Neil hadn't experienced anything similar in reaction to his playacting. He opened his menu and began perusing it. Cara followed his example. Neither of them made any further mention of Agnes or paid her any further attention.

They ordered their meals. The waitress soon brought their salads and a basket of hot rolls. Cara ate with relish, enjoying the food and Neil's company. The conversation never hit a lull. The two of them always had things to talk about. Cara didn't bring up Roy's name, nor did Neil until the plates were cleared away and they were having coffee.

"You said you'd decided to break off with Xavier," he stated, stirring cream into his coffee.

"Yes, I had gotten up the courage to tell him last night, but he worked late, and we ended up just talking on the phone. So I put off telling him."

"Don't procrastinate, Cara. The sooner you stop the wedding preparations, the better for everybody."

"You're right." Cara sipped her coffee.

Neil frowned, obviously not satisfied with her answer. He leaned toward her and lowered his voice before he spoke in the same sober tone, "After our conversation today when you were leaving to go to the post office, I did some thinking. If you're going to marry anybody out of desperation just so Sophia can attend your wedding, I'd rather it be me." Cara was so taken by surprise and so humbled by this proof of his affection for her that she just gazed at him, tongue-tied. He went on, "Not that I'm in favor of the whole idea, mind you. And, of course, it wouldn't be a real marriage. We wouldn't sleep together, naturally." This last statement came out sounding stern. He sat upright again.

Cara felt herself blushing and wondered whether he'd been aware of how she'd responded earlier to his kissing her hand. "Neil, I'm deeply touched. This afternoon I wasn't proposing. Honest. I would never put you on the spot like that."

"I didn't construe what you said as a proposal. My offer is purely voluntary. Consider it a backup plan if you start wavering about breaking off with Xavier."

"Oh, I see. You're afraid I'm too big a coward to face the music."

"You're under a lot of pressure. Don't be hard on yourself." He reached over and gave her forearm a gentle squeeze. Cara felt a warm tingle of pleasure in his touch. Warm pleasure had always been there when Neil patted or hugged her, but the tingle was new. What was going on?

"My conscience wouldn't allow me to exploit our friendship," she said and sipped her coffee. "We're talking a major disruption of your life."

He shrugged. "I have a routine more than I have a life." The statement was quietly matter-of-fact. He wasn't asking for pity, but Cara felt a surge of compassion anyway as she thought of how lonely he must be.

"You haven't dated at all, have you?" she asked.

"No. I wouldn't make a very good date."

"Tell that to all the women who come on to you. Some of them even ask you to go out. I've heard you let them down easy." She hesitated. "It's been three years, Neil. You don't want to live alone indefinitely."

"Between work and my involvement in civic organizations, I have a lot of interaction with people. Don't make me out to be a hermit. How did the conversation get on to me, anyway? We were discussing you."

Cara wrinkled up her nose. "Aren't we always?"

"So you'll take steps to stop the wedding? Tomorrow?"

"Tomorrow. I'll invite Roy over to my place for supper and tell him I can't go through with marrying him. Then the hard part." She sighed. "Breaking the news to Nonna and my mother. They'll inform the rest of the family. My best bet is to take my phone off the hook. Better yet, leave town until the worst blows over.''

''Tell your family you're acting on my advice. Make me out to be the bad guy. I can take the flack.''

''You're so sweet.''

The waitress brought the check. Cara asked if she could pay half and he said no. While he was taking out his wallet and extracting a credit card, she glanced over and noted that Agnes Tanner and her husband had departed. Cara hadn't noticed them leaving. She hadn't been aware of anybody except Neil all through dinner, for that matter. Their table might have been a private island in the room.

Poor Roy. She'd never been that focused on him when the two of them were out together in public. For the first time, Cara was willing to admit that maybe Roy had had a legitimate complaint about her devotion to her boss.

No more was said about Neil's willingness to participate in a fake marriage, but Cara knew without a single doubt he would stand by his word if she decided to take him up on the offer. The knowledge that he'd given her what he called a ''back up plan'' would, she knew, shore up her courage to act decisively—and wisely—in rectifying the mistake she'd made in accepting Roy's proposal. That had been Neil's intention—to push her in the right direction.

The scene with Roy the next evening turned out to be much uglier than Cara could ever have imagined.

It turned out to be much briefer, too. They never got around to eating the meal she'd prepared. Roy was in a fury when he arrived and began hurling bitter accusations about her fooling around with her boss behind Roy's back.

Cara could barely get in a word, but she quickly surmised that Agnes Tanner had been busy spreading gossip, and Roy had gotten a full-blown account of yesterday's embrace outside the store and last night's innocent playacting at the restaurant.

"I've had it up to here!" Roy shouted, with a slashing motion across his throat. "The wedding's off!"

"I'm so sorry about all this," Cara began in a contrite tone.

He didn't let her continue a meek explanation. "So it's okay with you to call the wedding off?" he demanded.

Cara sighed in defeat and nodded. The whole story was so complicated, and what could she say to salve his pride? "I'm truly sorry, Roy. And I don't blame you for being angry."

"Spare me any apologies, you—" He balled up his fist, and for one frightened second, Cara cowered away from him, afraid he might strike her. He conquered the violent impulse and instead directed a tirade of verbal abuse at her before he stormed out.

The loud slamming of the door made Cara wince. She collapsed into a chair, weak with relief and horrified that she might actually have married Roy, a potential wife-beater, judging from the way he'd acted tonight. Ironically, his language and his behavior absolved her of a great deal of guilt. He didn't love her, either, because no man who loved a woman could call her such foul names and accuse her of such sleazy actions. Roy's mind was in the gutter.

"No wonder Neil took a dislike to him," Cara murmured.

One thing for sure—she wouldn't describe the breakup scene to Neil in any great detail. He just might call Roy up or, worse, go to see him and bawl him out for treating Cara as he had. Neil had come to her defense in the past. Cara remembered a couple of incidents during her teens when he'd tracked down boys who'd acted disrespectfully toward her. She didn't know what he'd said or done, but he'd cured the problem in each case.

The phone was ringing. Cara rose and picked up the cordless phone from an end table. She spoke a cautious hello. Roy could be calling to shout at her some more or any number of friends could be checking in to report the rumors Agnes was circulating.

"Cara Marie." Her mother's voice came over the line. Cara's heart sank. She could easily picture Rose LaCroix's face, her compressed lips and grim expression. The gossip must have made it to her ears already.

"Hi, Mamma. How are you?"

Rose ignored her conversational opener. "Are you talking on that cordless phone?"

"Why, yes."

"I don't want the whole world listening in to what I have to say, even if it is a pack of lies."

Recently there had been a feature on the local news about the lack of privacy in using cell phones and cordless phones. The news reporter had played recordings of intercepted conversations, some of them embarrassingly personal.

"Why don't I come over in about fifteen minutes?" Cara said. She might as well go ahead and finish the job of calling a halt to the wedding preparations. Especially since nosy Agnes had laid the groundwork.

"We'll be here. Your daddy is at a meeting," Rose added.

So "we" meant Rose and Sophia, Cara deduced, the dread settling over her like a heavy blanket and making her clumsy as she hurriedly put the uneaten dinner in plastic containers to stow in the refrigerator. *My stomach feels hollow, but I'm not even hungry. That's a first,* she thought, wiping up spillage on the counter.

The drive to her parents' house took her only ten minutes. She parked in the driveway and entered through the rear porch, as was her habit. It wasn't necessary to use her key since the doors weren't locked and wouldn't be locked until bedtime.

"We're in here. In the kitchen," Rose called out.

Cara inhaled the mouthwatering aroma of food. The worst case of nerves couldn't deaden her tastebuds to her mother's cooking. "I smell something delicious."

Sophia spoke up, "Stuffed manicotti. Your mamma

is heating some up for you in the microwave oven in case you didn't eat supper yet.''

None of Rose's children could err badly enough to kill her nurturing instincts. That knowledge gave Cara some slight reassurance.

"I haven't eaten," she said from the doorway. Rose stood by the counter, a pot holder in either hand. Sophia sat at the table, wearing a robe, looking thin and gaunt and ever so dear.

"Sit down here, next to me, *cara mia.*" Sophia patted the seat of the chair adjacent to hers.

Cara went over and hugged her grandmother and kissed her on the cheek before she did as instructed. Rose set down a plate in front of her. "You want iced tea?" she asked.

"Please."

"Eat," Sophia scolded. "It's good."

Cara picked up her fork. "Thanks, Mamma," she said when Rose served the glass of iced tea.

"You're welcome." Rose sat down across from them, her hands firmly clasped in front of her. Cara knew better than to expect a reprieve while she was eating, and, sure enough, her mother came right to the point. "So who's spreading these lies about you fooling around with your boss behind Roy's back?"

"How did you hear?"

"Angela from next door came over, all embarrassed, and told me it was the big topic of conversation at the Ladies' Altar Circle meeting this afternoon. She thought I ought to know. No sooner had she gone than your Aunt Mary called to say the story was all over Hammond. I gave her a piece of my mind when she asked me if there was any truth to it. Then she had the gall to say she hoped the wedding was still on. I said, 'Of course, it is,' and made an excuse and hung up.''

Mary Landry was Cara's father's sister, and no love was lost between her and Rose, as Cara well knew.

Sophia smoothed the placemat in front of her with a bony, fragile hand. ''Poor Mary's always been jealous because you had pretty daughters and her girls are so plain, Rose. It wouldn't surprise me if she started the gossip herself out of pure spite.''

Cara laid down her fork. ''Aunt Mary didn't start the gossip. I'm guessing Agnes Tanner is behind it. She was at the same restaurant last night where Neil and I went to have dinner.''

Rose's brown eyes grew as round as marbles. ''Cara Marie,'' she said in a shocked tone. ''You don't go out on dates with other men when you're engaged to be married.''

''Neil isn't 'other men.' I've known him forever.''

''Where was Roy? Where is he tonight?''

''Last night he was at his regular poker game. And tonight he came to my apartment. He'd heard the gossip, too, and believed it. We had a big fight and broke up.''

''She broke up with her fiancé, Mamma. Did you hear that? There's going to be no wedding.''

''I heard,'' Sophia replied. To Cara's anxious eye,

her grandmother seemed to shrink and grow more frail. Sophia had regained some of her old animation during the past few weeks since Cara had announced her engagement. Now that animation had died.

Rose sat with her palm clapped across her forehead and her eyes closed, reciting a quick prayer.

"I'm so sorry," Cara said. "I realized a few days ago that I couldn't marry Roy. I don't love him, and he insisted I give up my job...."

Sophia patted her arm. "Finish your supper. Then come and tell your nonna good-night. I'm going to lie down and rest."

"But, Mamma, your favorite TV show is coming on," Rose said. "You want me to tape it for you?"

"Yes. I'll watch it tomorrow."

Cara wanted to burst out crying, but what good would that do? It wouldn't change the fact that she was the cause of the disappointment weighing down the atmosphere in the room. She *had* to do something, say something to dispel the gloom and revive the expectation she'd cruelly fostered in the first place. Her mother was healthy and could cope, but Nonna wasn't in good health.

Neil had given her permission to claim he was her new love interest, Cara reminded herself.

"Before you go to bed, Nonna, I have a secret to tell you and Mamma. Now don't you breathe a word to anyone. You swear?"

Rose and Sophia both leaned toward her.

"Those rumors about Neil and me? Well, there's some truth in them."

Chapter Four

It wasn't even necessary for Cara to embroider the fib—a fib being an untruth motivated by good, as compared to a lie—into a believable romance. Her mother and her grandmother did that for her.

"So that nice Griffin boy finally woke up!" Sophia exclaimed, a delighted smile breaking across her dear old face. "You always worshipped the ground he walked on."

"I'll bet you got his attention when you were about to marry another man," Rose said, nodding wisely. "He saw you were about to slip through his fingers."

"He realized our Cara is one of a kind." Sophia caressed Cara's cheek lovingly. "He won't find himself another wife so sweet and good."

Rose dealt with practicalities. "You'll want to wait a few weeks before you announce your engagement. Otherwise it would look odd, canceling one wedding and planning another one."

"Neil and I haven't actually discussed wedding dates," Cara put in weakly. She had only meant to lift their spirits, not obligate Neil to step in and replace Roy as bridegroom, even though he'd agreed to do so.

"God will understand the rush," Sophia stated, her tone tranquil. Seeing the change in her grandmother now that hope was reborn for Cara's future, Cara couldn't be sorry for the deception. God in His infinite wisdom surely would understand everything.

"I didn't really like that Roy Xavier all that much," Rose revealed. "He struck me as a typical car salesman, all phony smiles and handshakes. Your daddy agreed with me."

So did Sophia. So did Natalie and Angie and the majority of the family, Cara learned. No wonder Rose and Sophia had been so quick to accept Cara's breakup with Roy and new relationship with Neil.

The gabfest continued until Rose noted that it was almost time for Sophia's TV program. Cara declined the invitation to stay and watch it with them. After fond good-night hugs and kisses, she made her escape.

On the way to her car, she glanced toward the kitchen. Through a window she could see her mother standing at the wall phone, gesturing with her free hand while she carried on animated conversation. Rose hadn't even waited until Cara had backed out of the driveway to start spreading the highly secret news.

"I'd better warn Neil tonight. People may start congratulating him by tomorrow," Cara said aloud to herself and sighed. She hated to complicate his life like this. Especially since he'd given her sound advice when she was considering Roy's marriage proposal.

It was still early enough that Cara decided she'd rather explain in person to Neil what she'd gotten him into, rather than tell him on the phone. She drove directly to his house and saw lights on.

"Hi, Cara," he greeted her with a note of surprise when he opened the front door. He was dressed in jeans and a T-shirt, and wearing only socks on his feet.

"You're going to hate me," she declared.

His expression grew stern as he studied her face. "I'm not going to hate you, whatever you've done. Or not done. I thought you were having Xavier over for dinner tonight to call off the wedding."

"He came, all right, but he didn't eat dinner. He was too mad."

"You did break up with him?"

"Actually he broke up with me."

The tension seemed to ebb from his body, and his slight frown smoothed out. "Either way, I'm glad to hear it." He opened the door wide in a wordless invitation for her to come in.

Cara had been inside the house on other occasions. She walked ahead of him into the living room and went over to perch on a man-size brown tweed sofa, which, like the worn brown leather recliner, was a castoff from his parents' home. Cara had sat on the sofa in their den.

Neil hadn't brought any household belongings with him from Memphis when he moved back to Hammond following the death of his wife and son. He'd lived with Dean and Judith Griffin for a year, then bought this one-story brick house when they'd put their home up for sale, prior to relocating to Florida.

"Would you like a beer or a soft drink?" Neil inquired. "That's about all I have to offer you to drink, other than coffee or tea."

"Nothing, thanks. I just had iced tea at Mamma's house." The TV was playing. He'd obviously been watching a TV program.

He looked thoughtful, registering the information that she'd come to see him after visiting her parents and Sophia.

"Do you want to sit down?" Cara asked nervously, curbing the urge to blurt out a confession.

"Sure." Neil picked up the remote from the square wooden coffee table and clicked off the TV before he sat down on the sofa, too. "Okay. Out with it," he said.

She breathed in and breathed out. "You know that backup plan you gave me last night? That you would marry me, in a pinch?"

"Yes."

"Well, I set it in motion. Not intentionally. I only meant to use the make-believe romance part, but my mother and Nonna jumped to conclusions." Cara lifted her hands in a helpless gesture. "I didn't have the heart to correct them. Here's what happened." She filled him in, talking fast and interjecting frequent apologies. "I'm so sorry," she said once again when she'd run out of explanation.

"Don't take all the blame," Neil chided her. He slid closer and put his arm around her shoulders and gave her a supportive hug. "I'm at fault, too, for putting on a show for Agnes Tanner at the restaurant. Dammit, I didn't stop and think about the harmful consequences of egging her on. Thanks to me, your family has suffered embarrassment. And Xavier, too."

Cara might have known that Neil would assume his share of responsibility and more. Of all the people in the world, including her family, he was the person she could depend on most to stand behind her. Gratitude welled up that he hadn't made her feel even worse than she already did. "Neither of us meant to hurt anybody," she pointed out, laying her head on his shoulder.

"You're much too soft-hearted to do anything mean or spiteful," he said stoutly in her defense.

"But look at the awful mess I've gotten you into."

"We'll get through it together."

Cara kissed him on the cheek, wordlessly telling him Thank you and I'm sorry.

Neil hugged her close, and Cara hugged him back, feeling guilty over the fact that, despite the terrible predicament she'd created for them both, she was perfectly happy and content to be sitting there on his sofa in his living room. More content than she'd ever been when Roy embraced her during the brief period when they were engaged to be married. Safe and protected in Neil's arms, it was difficult to muster anxiety and self-reproach. He'd always fostered the belief in her that everything would be okay.

"I'm not much of an actor," Neil said. "That's what bothers me." His troubled tone burst Cara's bubble of well-being, reviving her regret over disrupting his life. She easily followed his train of thought: it wouldn't be easy for him to act like her lover, when he'd been like a brother to her for so many years.

"You fooled Agnes Tanner easily enough in the restaurant last night with your Casanova imitation," she reminded him. The memory came back of how his playacting had affected Cara, arousing that tingle of delight. Would repetition of lover-like attentions dull the reaction, or would she experience it again and again? The question worried Cara. A lot. Later she would test it out, using her imagination. But not now. Not here with Neil.

"Agnes is no challenge since, like most gossips, she seems to always be looking for the worst qualities in other human beings," he was replying. "It's a different matter with people who know us well, like Jimmy and Peewee."

"And Allison and Mary Ann..." Cara's voice drifted off on a note of dismay as she added to the list of her co-workers, and his employees, at the store.

"Gosh, I can't stand the thought of deliberately misleading them, can you?" She raised her head as Neil's arms loosened. He sat further apart from her until they were back in their original positions.

"No, but we'll have to."

"I should just go back to my parents' house right now and tell them I just made up the whole thing, out of desperation."

"You can't do that. Think about how disappointed Sophia will be."

Cara slumped lower as she visualized her grandmother's reaction to the truth. The joy fading away and expectation dying. "You're right," she whispered. "I just can't. It would be too cruel."

Neil squeezed her shoulder as though to say, End of subject. "Our best bet is to make a game plan and stick to it. Tomorrow morning I'll hold a short staff meeting, and we'll deal with the gossip head-on. We'll announce that you've called off your marriage to Xavier. I'll state simply that I realized I couldn't let another man steal you from under my nose. We'll hint strongly that there may be another wedding in the not-so-distant future. Yours and mine."

They sat there in silence for a full minute at least. Cara assumed he was imagining the meeting, too, perhaps rehearsing his words, as she was doing.

"It'll work," he said. "We can carry this off."

"Sure, we can." Another worrisome complication occurred to Cara. "What about your parents? Since they're off in Florida, can't we confide in them?"

Neil shook his head after only the slightest hesitation. "Too risky. My mother keeps in touch with some of her good friends here in Hammond. She would end up letting the cat out of the bag, swearing her friends to secrecy."

"You're right. Which means your parents will make a special trip here to attend our wedding." Cara sighed, her spirits weighed down by all the repercussions of well-intentioned dishonesty.

They talked a while longer, and then she got up to leave. Neil walked with her to the door, where he gave her a good-night hug. Cara stood on tiptoe to kiss him on the cheek, but she stopped herself and dropped back on her heels.

"I guess we should rehearse, shouldn't we?" she asked timidly, ignoring the fluttering of her pulse.

"Rehearse?"

"What if one of your neighbors saw us saying good-night? They would think it odd if I gave you a peck on the cheek, like I always do."

Neil didn't answer. Cara's heart took a strange leap as his gaze dropped to her lips. He was processing the idea of her kissing him on the mouth instead.

"We're safe tonight," he stated, drawing back a partial step. "The only neighbors with a view of my front door are the Carters across the street, and they're out of town."

"But they'll come back."

"Okay. Let's pretend they're peeking out from behind a curtain," Neil said lightly, humoring her. He bent and gave her a quick chaste kiss on the lips. "Drive carefully. I'll see you at the store tomorrow."

Cara mumbled an answer and turned away to walk to her car. She found her own disappointment extremely disturbing. What did she expect from Neil? Not passion. It wasn't as if she wanted him to desire her. Or did she?

This is crazy, Neil thought as he closed the door after Cara's car had disappeared from sight. He and Cara, husband and wife? When he'd agreed to a sham marriage, he hadn't really believed for a moment that she'd choose that route. Why, marrying him was almost like her marrying an older stepbrother.

There was no backing out. He'd given her the option and she'd taken it out of sheer desperation. *Better you as a temporary bridegroom than Xavier,* Neil reflected and felt somewhat better, taking that angle. His motive from the first had been protecting Cara. He could see to it that she was unscathed by the whole experience.

The part that bothered him was posing as her lover. That smacked of impropriety. Neil's deep affection for Cara was platonic, not sexual. He'd never allowed himself to indulge in secret lust, not even when he was eighteen and she'd suddenly developed a lush figure at the age of thirteen. Neil had kept a mental barrier firmly in place, and he meant to continue to keep it in place. When this fake marriage was over, he wanted his friendship with Cara to have remained intact. She was as important to him as his own flesh and blood.

What Cara needed to realize was that Neil wasn't made out of stone. He couldn't kiss those pouty, sexy lips of her like a man kisses a woman he's dating and not *feel* something carnal. Sooner or later—and probably sooner—Neil guessed he would have to initiate a frank discussion.

In his living room he settled in the recliner with the TV remote and flipped channels, finding none of the programs interesting enough to watch. *Better enjoy your channel surfing for the next few weeks,* he told himself. Cara would be moving in with him for the duration of their temporary marriage, and she would have a vote on what programs they watched when they both were home at night.

Neil imagined the two of them sitting in the living room, him sprawled in the chair and her relaxed on the sofa. The scene was nice. Very nice.

On his way to bed, Neil paused in the hallway and pushed open the door to the spare bedroom, which was furnished with more of his parents' castoffs. Queen-size bed. Dresser. Chest of drawers. Even the bedspread and curtains had been donated by his mother.

Neil figured he would take this room for himself and give Cara the master bedroom with its own bath and a walk-in closet. She could pick out a new bedspread, something more feminine. He would gladly hang new curtains for her, too. Hell, he wouldn't balk at new carpet.

The whole house could use some sprucing up, for that matter. Neil hadn't even repainted the walls when he bought the place. He hadn't really cared about the color scheme. Hadn't cared about creating a homey atmosphere. Cara undoubtedly saw the house interior as stark and drab. Because it *was* stark and drab. *I could repaint the other rooms, too, and put down new carpet,* Neil reflected.

True, Cara would only be making his house her temporary home. Still Neil wanted her to be happy and comfortable while she stayed with him.

"I'm nervous," Cara whispered.

"Don't be. Everything will be okay." Neil took her hand and gave it a reassuring squeeze. He kept her there close beside him while he addressed his assembled employees, all looking mildly curious as they perched on high stools at the long counter or stood waiting to hear why the boss had called an impromptu staff meeting ten minutes before the store opened to business.

Neil came right to the point. "You may have heard some gossip circulating about Cara and me."

A couple of heads nodded. Allison Pendergast spoke up hesitantly, "Two people called me last night to ask if it was true that Cara and Roy Xavier broke up. They'd heard rumors that you and Cara were seen holding hands at the Forest Restaurant."

Cara responded before Neil could. "It's true that Roy and I have called off our wedding. So feel free to confirm that rumor, everybody.'' She looked from one face to another and, surprisingly, read no sympathy or dismay on her behalf. Hadn't anybody thought she and Roy were a good match?

"And it's also true that Cara and I held hands a couple of nights ago at the Forest,'' said Neil. "In fact, you can confirm to anyone that asks that we're an 'item.''' He slipped his arm around Cara's waist, casually staking possession. "I finally woke up to the reason I was so opposed to her getting married. I was jealous as hell.''

Cara felt her cheeks flush with the little thrill of pleasure his words awoke, even though she knew he wasn't being honest about the jealousy motive. "We wanted each of you to know the situation right away,'' she said.

"Well, I'm all for it!'' Allison declared with a broad smile. "Congratulations, you two!''

"Yeah, congratulations!'' said Jimmy, and the others each had some pleased, sincere comment. No one looked stunned or even greatly surprised. There wasn't a hint of skepticism in the air, to Cara's relief and amazement.

"We're just dating for now,'' she put in hastily when she had the chance.

"Still, I think I'll wait a while to return my wedding present I just bought,'' said Allison, smirking.

"Please don't hold on to it,'' Cara begged. "If Neil and I decide to get married, we won't need a thing to set up house. Will we, Neil?'' She met his gaze im-

ploringly. Wedding presents! Another detail she hadn't
even considered: accepting gifts under false pretenses.

"No, between us, Cara and I already have all the
necessities."

Mary Ann Hoffman, who worked in the office with
Cara and Allison, batted her hand at him. "'Necessities!' Just like a man to be so practical. I'm keeping
what I bought, too, because it's not a 'necessity.'"

"Hey, is the meeting over?" asked Peewee. "I see
customers already pulling up outside."

"Yes, the meeting's over." Neil clapped his hands
together smartly. "Let's sell some merchandise."

As the group dispersed, there were joking comments
about his needing to make a big success of his business now more than before. Obviously everybody expected the new romance between him and Cara to
blossom and end in marriage. A happy marriage.

How Cara hated deceiving her co-workers. Then she
pictured her grandmother's face and salved her conscience with the reminder: there was a good reason.
An unselfish reason.

And nobody would be hurt.

Chapter Five

"How about a movie tomorrow night?" Neil made the suggestion at lunch on Friday.

Cara was instantly enthusiastic about the idea. "I'd love to go to a movie. Why don't we see that thriller they've been advertising constantly on TV with Julia Roberts and Sean Connery as undercover FBI agents? Or maybe there's another movie you have in mind," she added when he didn't respond right away.

"No, that one's probably a good choice. It looks action-packed from the advertisement."

"You're sure?"

"I'm sure."

The conversation lapsed while their waitress refilled their iced-tea glasses.

"This is so much *fun* I feel guilty," Cara confided once she'd gone. "Lunch out at a restaurant every day, supper together most nights at your place or mine or at a different restaurant. And now a movie date."

His smile held indulgence. "We're supposed to be dating."

"Yes, but should I be having this good a time at pretending? And it's costing you a fortune." He'd steadfastly refused her offers to pay her share.

"No, it isn't. Besides, I can afford the expense."

"You *are* having fun, too?"

"Don't I seem to be enjoying myself?" he chided her.

"Yes."

"Well, I am."

She smiled, happy to take him at his word. "Good." Her real courtship with Roy hadn't been nearly this enjoyable for her.

The movie was showing at the new stadium theatre in Hammond. Cara called and got the show times when she returned to the store. In a conversation with Allison, she learned that her co-worker and her husband, Greg, were also planning to see the same movie the following night.

"Don't worry. We won't sit by you two lovebirds," Allison promised, her tone teasing. "It would make me nostalgic, seeing you hold hands and steal kisses like Greg and I used to do before we got married. Now all we do is shovel popcorn into our mouths."

As things turned out, Allison didn't keep her promise not to sit by Cara and Neil at the movie theatre. She and Greg arrived barely a minute before the lights dimmed. By then the theatre was full almost to capacity, and they were more than glad to find two empty seats next to Cara.

"Sorry," Allison apologized. "The sitter was late."

"Don't be silly," Cara said. "We don't mind a bit." But she did feel self-conscious. Allison wouldn't be keeping a watch on Cara and Neil, but she would expect them to behave like a couple who were dating, not like old friends.

Cara waited nervously during the first preview for Neil to initiate some hand-holding. When he didn't, she decided she would have to take the lead herself. Shifting her weight, she rested her shoulder against his. He looked at her questioningly. She smiled and mouthed Allison's name. He nodded, but still seemed puzzled. Cara obviously needed to make her message clearer that they needed to act romantic.

She leaned closer and kissed him on the mouth. His quick intake of breath was audible to her, even over the soundtrack of the second preview. Cara's heartbeat had picked up speed, and her skin felt flushed. She wanted to kiss him again and this time let her lips linger against his, savor the texture and warmth of his lips. The impulse had nothing to do with Allison.

Now you kiss me, she urged him silently. For a breathtaking second, she thought he would grant her wish, but instead he drew in another sharp breath and briefly closed his eyes. Cara directed her gaze at the screen, disappointed. Neil took her hand and squeezed it, then threaded his fingers through hers and brought her hand over onto his thigh. He was doing his part to act like a lover. Or a would-be lover.

That had been his bargain, Cara reminded herself. To *pretend* to desire her. It wasn't his fault that she was beginning to want the real thing.

The movie started. Soon Cara thought she understood why Neil hadn't jumped at the idea of seeing this particular film. Maybe he'd read a review and knew more about the plot than she had. Not only were the two main characters undercover agents but a part of their "cover" was the fiction that they were man and wife. From the first scene when they were alone together in a motel room, the physical attraction sizzled between them.

"Baby, this movie makes me hot," Allison murmured to Greg in the middle of a scene where the two agents made passionate love in the shower. Cara surmised from Neil's sideways glance in Allison's direction that he'd also overheard the earthy comment.

Me, too, Cara could have said. Her hand felt sweaty in Neil's grasp, which tightened and loosened with his own tension. His thigh felt hard as a rock, and he twitched restlessly in his chair. Did he find the movie arousing, like she did, or did it just make him uncomfortable? Cara wondered.

"Gosh, that was great! Wasn't it?" Allison demanded when the credits were rolling. "A chick flick and a guy flick, all rolled up into one!"

Greg and Cara and Neil all responded affirmatively. Cara would swear that Neil's voice held pained relief, and he bolted up out of his chair when they stood up.

Outside, the other couple said their goodbyes and hurried toward their car, arm in arm. "You pay the baby-sitter when we get home, and I'll—" Allison lowered her voice so that the rest of the sentence couldn't be heard, but their laughter drifted back, hinting of intimate plans.

"How about coffee and dessert?" Neil asked.

"No dessert for me. Why don't we go to my place, and I'll make coffee?"

His refusal was quick. "That's too much trouble. And I have my mouth set for a piece of pie."

"Oh. Okay." He rarely ate sweets. Was the piece of pie simply an excuse to go to a public place and avoid being alone with her? Maybe he was afraid she would come on to him. The speculation brought a flush of embarrassment because Cara would have liked to do just that once she got him alone.

"You really did like the movie?" she asked in the car.

"It was a good flick."

"But—" She prompted him to put into the words the reservation in his comment.

He seemed to hesitate. "I could have done with more action and less explicit sex. Especially considering the storyline."

"You mean their posing as married people. There wasn't much parallel with our situation. For one thing,

I'm not gorgeous and sexy, like Julia Roberts.'' Cara hadn't meant to sound wistful. ''And I'm not fishing for compliments,'' she said quickly when Neil shot her a look.

''You're prettier than Julia Roberts, in my book.''

But not sexy, in his book. She eased out a sigh. ''Thank you. You're very sweet.''

Cara let the conversation lapse.

At the restaurant Neil ordered coffee for them both, but no pie for himself.

''What about your pie?'' she asked.

''I think I'll pass since you're not having dessert.''

Cara bit her lip, but decided she would bust if she didn't say what was on her mind. ''You didn't really want pie, did you? Next time, just be honest, Neil. Okay? You don't have to handle me with kid gloves. Just give it to me straight. 'Cara, I'd feel safer not going to your place where you might make a pass at me.' ''

'' 'Give it to you straight,' '' he repeated, his tone grim. She could see the ridges of his jaw muscles. ''All right. Here goes. It's been three years since I made love. I'm human. I need your cooperation, Cara, if we're going to get through this marriage business without ending up in bed together. Dammit, I want us to still be friends when it's all over. Don't you?''

The raw frustration in his voice and eyes rendered her speechless for a second or two. Cara swallowed and found her voice. ''I want us to be friends always.''

"Then keep that goal in mind. Don't play sex kitten."

"'Sex kitten'!" She was as offended as she was taken aback. "You think I was being seductive in the movie when I kissed you? Well, I wasn't doing any such thing. I just knew Allison expected us to act romantic, and you just sat there, like my brother!"

"I *am* like a brother to you. I picked you up off the sidewalk when you were bawling at the top of your lungs because you'd fallen off your tricycle. I wiped your nose when you had a cold. I took you to the bathroom more than once, for Pete's sakes."

"I remember all that.... And I love you for it."

"I love you, too. Like a brother." He enunciated the last three words for emphasis.

Cara was moved deeply by his simple statement of his love, which never had been in question. Her emotions demanded that she be completely honest with him. "The problem is that my feelings *aren't* entirely sisterly toward you. They never were entirely sisterly. I was always envious of your girlfriends, whereas I didn't envy Tony's girlfriends. Or Michael's girlfriends."

He closed his eyes and gave his head a shake, rejecting her admission as even a topic of discussion. "Our deal was a marriage in name only. So that Sophia could attend your wedding."

"Yes, that was our deal." Cara was filled with contrition that she was paying him back for his kindness by not abiding by his ground rules. "I'm sorry, Neil. I'll try my best to be good from now on. I promise."

The waitress came with the coffee. While they were being served, Cara scraped up all her courage. "Could I ask you one thing before we close the subject?" she asked as soon as the woman had gone.

He was tearing open a packet of sugar and let his silence serve as cautious permission.

"If it weren't for your mental block against the idea of being attracted to me sexually, would you be...tempted?"

Neil picked up the cream pitcher and dumped most of the contents into his coffee. "I'm not going to answer that." He stirred his coffee so hard the pale liquid sloshed out of the over-full cup.

"Oh. Okay." Cara tore open a packet of low-calorie sweetener. Was his agitation a form of a yes answer? Or just annoyance? She had no way of finding out and still keeping her promise. "So how are we going to handle our public relationship? We can't behave like brother and sister and expect people, including my family, to believe we're madly in love, can we?"

"No. My point is that putting on a show won't be a problem as long as we ourselves keep the line drawn between pretense and reality."

"Don't get caught up in the pretense, in other words."

"Exactly."

"And don't start wishing it wasn't pretense."

He looked at her with exasperation. "Cara." Her name was spoken as a reproof.

"Sorry," she said glumly. "I'll try hard, Neil. I really will, if it kills me."

"Let me take the lead, okay?"

"Okay."

"And we don't have to be overly demonstrative in public. Personally, I find that to be in bad taste."

"Me, too."

He drew in a deep breath and expelled it. "Good. I'm glad we're on the same wavelength."

Cara sipped her coffee and resolved that she would honestly try to be on the same wavelength. After all, Neil was doing her a tremendous favor. The least she could do was make the experience of fake courtship and temporary marriage as painless for him as possible.

Besides, she certainly didn't want to undermine their friendship. If Neil were to change his attitude... But he wasn't likely to. Cara dismissed that dreamy line of thought.

Neil hadn't seen Cara's grandmother for quite some time. Perhaps a year. Even though he'd expected some signs of illness, her changed appearance still came as a shock. She'd always been a stout, robust woman. The weight had melted away, and she was thin now and looked fragile. Her handsome features seemed large for her face.

One thing hadn't changed, though. Sophia still

doted on her youngest granddaughter. Every time her gaze lit on Cara, a smile came to her lips, and her sunken dark-brown eyes glowed with love and pride.

Neil had understood before today the urgency Cara felt to grant her ill grandmother's wish to see Cara happily married before she died. In Sophia's presence here at the LaCroix home on a Sunday, he comprehended that urgency even better. The closeness of grandmother and granddaughter was something beautiful to witness.

His own affection and concern for Cara had led Neil to agree to the fake marriage, but he found himself feeling glad that he could play a role in brightening Sophia's last weeks and months on earth.

"So, Neil, when are you going to put an engagement ring on our Cara's finger?" Sophia directed this blunt question to him in the living room following a hearty meal of lasagne. Neil and Cara had been the only company, at Cara's request, Neil knew.

"Nonna! You're embarrassing me!" Cara admonished, blushing prettily.

Her father, seated in his recliner, chuckled, and Rose LaCroix, observing from her platform rocker, tittered.

"Good question," Neil said. "No time better than the present, I've always heard." Suppressing a grin, he dug into his pocket and brought out a tiny velvet pouch he'd gotten from the jeweler. Even a small box would have been too noticeable in his slacks pocket.

"What on *earth?*" Cara burst out. "Neil, you *didn't!*"

He grinned a confession. "I did."

"We discussed an engagement ring, and I told you not to buy one."

"Hush, Cara," chided Sophia, who sat with her veined old hands clasped together like a child delighted over a surprise. "Rose, you didn't teach your daughter good manners."

"You spoiled her, Mamma." Rose LaCroix was all smiles.

Watched closely by four pairs of eyes, Neil took the ring out of the bag. A mute Cara gave him her left hand, and he slipped the ring on.

"It's beautiful...." she breathed, gazing at her hand with an enthralled expression. "But..."

Neil kissed her on the lips to cut off the protest.

"Oh, *so* romantic," Sophia said. "Let me look closer with these old eyes at your engagement ring, Cara."

Rose had gotten up from her chair and even Basil LaCroix was leaning forward, looking pleased as punch. All of a sudden, Neil was stabbed by regret that the celebration wasn't genuine, that Cara wasn't really his fiancée, and her parents weren't really his future in-laws. Fortunately, no one noticed his momentary gravity. The attention was all focused on Cara and her ring.

Sophia's excitement and pleasure eased most of his guilt over deceiving these good people he'd known his entire life. No harm was being done, and the good outweighed the wrong. Neil regained his perspective and accepted the hearty congratulations.

"I can't believe you actually went to a jewelry store and bought a ring on the sly!"

"You wouldn't agree to a ring," Neil reminded her. He started the engine of his pickup. They'd just said their goodbyes and were leaving.

"Because I didn't want you to spend all that money."

"You know darned well I would look like a cheapskate not giving you an engagement ring."

He glanced over and smiled indulgently. She was holding up her hand and gazing at her ring finger, seeming every bit as enthralled as she had earlier when he'd slipped the ring on. "You seem to like it," he said.

"*Like* it? I *love* it. It's the engagement ring of my dreams. Emerald-cut diamond with baguette diamonds on either side. The problem is going to be taking it off and giving it back."

"The ring's yours for keeps."

"No way. I couldn't possibly keep it."

Neil didn't argue the point. He'd bought the ring for her and had no intention of accepting it back.

"Why didn't you give me some forewarning?" she asked. "I was completely dumbfounded when you reached into your pocket and brought out the little velvet pouch."

"I figured some drama might be good for you and me both when we made our wedding announcement. Your surprise was so genuine that it made our engagement more believable." He grinned. "Plus I kind of enjoyed your reaction."

"You'd just better watch your step. I'll get you back if it takes me ten years." She pinched him playfully on his arm.

Neil grabbed her hand, making some teasing reply. Before he realized what he was doing, he'd brought her hand up to his lips. Instead of kissing her knuckles, one by one, as he'd been about to do, he nipped her soft skin gently with his teeth and then released her hand.

After that, Neil pretended to be giving all his attention to driving. He was sobered by the realization that for a moment there, he'd felt unbelievably happy, caught up in the light-hearted mood that had once been the norm for him—until tragedy had struck three years ago.

It didn't seem right to be happy and complete when he was a widower and a bereaved father. Aside from the guilt, Neil wouldn't ever again feel safe being happy. It left you wide open for life to mow you down.

Another reason—maybe the *main* reason?—the marriage to Cara could only be a marriage in name only. If he were her husband in reality, he would love her heart and soul the same way he'd loved Lisa. Call him a coward, but Neil wasn't traveling that route again.

He'd already buried one wife, one child. He just couldn't live minute to minute, day to day, with the fear, the anxiety that fate would take a second swing at him.

Chapter Six

"What time will the shower be over?" asked Neil. He and Cara were touching base by phone on Saturday, two weeks before the wedding.

"Probably about five. Six at the latest." Cara sighed. "Nobody paid me the slightest attention when I asked for no showers. It makes me feel *awful* opening gifts that my friends and family have bought with their hard-earned money."

"Aren't showers a good excuse for an all-female party? I know my mother always seemed to thrive on them."

Neil was obviously trying to make her look on the brighter side. Cara felt a burst of the love that seemed to get stronger and stronger every day. She saw more and more about his character and personality to admire. To love. Try as she might not to foster hope that this marriage would magically turn into a real, lasting marriage, she just couldn't help herself. He could so easily be her ideal husband, if only he would let himself.

But he didn't *want* to be her husband, Cara reminded herself for the zillionth time. He was determined to remain her best male friend, her surrogate brother. And she was honor-bound not to tempt him to desire her as a woman.

There were signs, though, that he was having a struggle....

''I can tell you're distracted,'' he said, breaking into her thoughts. ''I'll hang up now and see you later. About six o'clock?''

He was coming over for supper and a work evening. They would pack up boxes to be put in storage during that period, however long it lasted, that she shared his house with him as Mrs. Neil Griffin. Instead of selling her town house, she was taking his advice and leasing it.

''I'm certain to be home by six,'' she assured him.

Cara was true to her word, but just barely. He'd parked his pickup and was getting out when she pulled in.

Neil walked over. ''Hi,'' he greeted her. ''The shower must have turned out to be fun.''

Cara made some answer and raised her face for his

usual chaste kiss that made a mockery of the gifts in boxes and gift bags piled on her back seat.

He leaned down and looked through the car window. "Do you have the rest of the loot in the trunk?"

"No, that's all the presents."

"Not much of a haul, compared to the last shower."

It had been a shower for general household items, some of which were bulkier than today's presents, but Cara didn't say that. She didn't want to get into explanations and encourage questions.

"Fewer people were invited to this one."

"Oh. Okay." He reached for the handle of the rear passenger door, obviously intending to help her carry the boxes and gift bags inside.

"Don't bother," she said quickly. "I'll take care of this stuff later." She wanted to leave the gifts outside for now. The memory of opening them up at the shower and responding to comments brought a blush to her cheeks.

"I might as well carry an armload in, since I'm standing here," Neil said reasonably. He gathered up a tall stack of boxes. Standing upright again, he hefted them. "Damn, these are light as a feather. What kind of shower was this anyway?"

The question he hadn't asked before now flustered Cara even more than she was already flustered. Pretending she hadn't heard, she leaned into the car and grabbed gift bags and an assortment of odd-size boxes. In her hurry, she was clumsy.

"Careful—"

Neil's admonition came too late. Two boxes and a bag were already tumbling out onto the pavement, spilling their silky contents. Cara froze, sensing his shock. She stole a quick glance at his face and saw that he was staring at the lacy garments exposed to view. Matching bra and panties in pale yellow, a sheer white nightgown with spaghetti straps and a champagne-colored teddy.

"It was a lingerie shower," she blurted. After freeing her hands by dropping all her packages onto the back seat again, she bent down and hastily stuffed the intimate apparel back into their original packaging.

"*That's* what's in all of these packages?" he asked, his voice strange. From the way he was now holding his stack of boxes, they might have contained explosives.

"I'm afraid so. You still want to take them inside?" She was meekly apologetic as well as embarrassed.

He actually hesitated, as though considering the option of replacing the boxes in her car. "Might as well if you're going to keep the stuff."

"What else can I do? Take it all to Goodwill? These presents didn't come from the dollar store."

"It's up to you what you do with them."

"We're talking outrageously expensive. You should see the nightgown and peignoir set my sisters gave me to wear on our wedding night. It's—"

He interrupted her, his tone brusque. "We can skip the description, if that's okay with you. And I definitely don't want to see any more than I've already seen. Coming?'' He headed for her town house.

By the time Cara had loaded herself up with what she could safely carry, his long strides had already taken him to her front door.

''It's not my fault this shower was given for me, Neil. I didn't ask for all these sexy, gorgeous underthings and sleepwear,'' she pointed out when she reached him.

''I'm not blaming you.''

''You seem to be blaming me. You're acting angry.''

Between her agitation and balancing her load, Cara had difficulty unlocking the door. ''Darn it!'' she muttered, fumbling with the keys.

Neil uttered a sound of frustration and said, ''Let me.''

He set his tall stack of boxes down roughly, the cardboard making a plopping sound on the tile. Cara moved aside, getting out of his way, and accidentally kicked the boxes. The stack toppled and a couple of lids flew off. Lingerie slithered out with a rustle of tissue paper.

''Oh, no! Look what I did!'' Cara wailed.

Neil did look, long and hard, before he turned his attention to jabbing the key in the lock. He was muttering curses under his breath. Cara had rarely known him to behave with such ill humor. After shoving the door open so hard it banged against the foyer wall, he stood there a second, obviously wracked by indecision about what to do next. One of his options might have been to leave immediately, judging from his glance past her toward his pickup.

"I'll come back and get the rest of this myself," Cara said, not wanting him to leave. "Let's go on inside." In addition to dismay over the whole fiasco, she was fascinated by seeing a side of him she'd never seen before. Neil never got this rattled over something minor.

Nor did he ever forget his Southern manners, but he charged on ahead of her, abandoning her on the doorstep in a most unchivalrous way.

Cara joined him in the living room after she'd finished stowing shower presents in a corner of her walk-in closet. She found him sitting on the sofa, TV remote gripped in his hand so tightly his knuckles showed white. He was gazing fixedly at the football action on her TV. When a commercial came on, he continued to stare with the same fierce concentration, confirming her guess that he wasn't really tuned in to the football game.

She sat down next to him and chided him in a gentle tone, "It's not that big a deal, Neil."

"I'm a normal man, Cara. I have a normal imagination."

Cara decided to ignore the second fierce statement, which she would really have liked to follow up on. "You're much nicer than the normal man. I'm sorry. I had no intention of showing you what I'd received at the shower." Even though she'd been wishing on the way home that she could do just that. "I didn't even tell you it was a lingerie shower because I didn't want to upset you."

"You're going to wear those nightgowns, that sexy, lacy underwear while we're living together? Is that playing fair?" he demanded.

She felt her face going warm, not just with embarrassment. He didn't mean the conversation to be titillating, but it was, for her. "I don't know what you thought I've been wearing underneath my clothes all these years, Neil, but I don't own any plain cotton bras and panties."

His gaze flicked over her figure. By the time he'd jerked his head aside, Cara's nipples were tingling and her whole body felt flushed.

"This is going to be pure hell," he said, shaking his head.

Cara's heart melted at his unhappy tone and expression. "It doesn't have to be. I'm more than willing to share a bedroom and make our marriage real." Substitute *eager* for *willing,* she thought.

"But I'm not," he stated soberly. "I never would have agreed to anything permanent. It wouldn't be fair to you, for any number of reasons."

"Such as?" His words had sliced through her like a sharp blade, making her want to cry. But she was determined not to let tears make the scene that much more painful for them both.

"Such as your desire to be a mother. You and

Xavier were going to start a family right away, you told me."

"Why is wanting kids a problem?" Cara had seen him with his son, and Neil had been a loving dad, not surprisingly. A dreadful thought occurred to her. "You didn't have a vasectomy, did you?"

"No, but I might as well have had one because I don't plan to be a father again, Cara. I've lost one child. I couldn't stand to go through that a second time."

Suddenly she understood so much she hadn't fully understood before. "Or stand to lose another wife you love."

"That either."

It wasn't grief alone or his memories of Lisa that had kept him from dating. He preferred to remain single indefinitely and cope with loneliness rather than risk being the victim of tragedy again.

"Call me a coward, and I won't argue," he said quietly.

"Don't be silly. I would never call you any derogatory name." Cara slid close and hugged him around his waist, laying her head on his shoulder. He hugged her back. In order to block out the awareness of her breasts pressing against his hard, muscular chest, she went back in time and remembered totally innocent hugs when she was a little girl.

Neil was employing the same technique. He'd been using it with increasing desperation the past couple of months, dredging up every image of her as a little girl stored away in his brain. But he couldn't control his subconscious when he fell asleep. He'd had sexy dreams about him and Cara that made him ashamed and angry at himself when he woke up, hotly aroused.

Seeing the sexy underthings and nightgowns wasn't going to make it any easier for him for to control this unwanted attraction to Cara. But that was his problem, not hers. She wasn't to blame for his hangups.

"Sorry for being such a horse's behind," he said gruffly, releasing her.

"You're forgiven." She kissed him on the cheek and got up from the sofa. "I'll go fix supper."

"Can I help?"

"No, the salad's already made. I just have to cook the spaghetti and warm up the meatballs and sauce. You relax a few minutes and watch the football game."

Neil needed a few minutes alone to collect himself. "You'll spoil me," he said.

She answered him over her shoulder as she was leaving the room. "I'm the one who's spoiled. You take me out to lunch almost every day and out to supper several times a week."

He settled back and actually did relax and watch the game. Soon a delectable aroma drifted from the kitchen, awakening his appetite. Contentment stole through him.

Neil had felt the same sense of well-being when he was married to Lisa. His happiness had seemed to insulate him from the tragedies that happened to other people.

Seemed to, but hadn't.

He'd learned how fleeting contentment and happiness could be. And how empty a life can become in the flash of an eye.

"I can't survive that again," he murmured aloud. "I really can't."

Cara didn't call out as she once would have done when she entered her parents' home without knocking on a Sunday afternoon. Back in those happy days before Sophia had been diagnosed with cancer, Cara could expect to find her parents and grandmother in the living room. Basil in his recliner, alternately dozing and watching TV, Rose in her platform rocker working the crossword puzzle in the newspaper, and Sophia on the sofa, crocheting, her feet comfortably propped on a hassock.

The last few months Cara's father often had the living room to himself when Cara visited. Sophia, who'd put away her crochet needles, spent more and more of her time in bed, resting, and Rose divided her attention between her husband and her ill mother.

Today Cara headed first toward the living room, intending to tell her father hello first before she went to Sophia's bedroom. She could hear the Saints game on the TV.

"Hi, Daddy..." Her voice died off. All three of them were seated in their places as though the clock had miraculously turned back. Her grandmother was wearing a house dress instead of a robe, and she was crocheting. A big lump formed in Cara's throat. With the greatest difficulty she kept her emotions under control and managed a bright smile as she made the rounds, kissing cheeks and responding to fond hellos.

"Why didn't you bring Neil with you?" Rose asked. "I hope he knows he doesn't need an invitation."

"I'm sure he does. He's at his house, tinkering with the old car he's restoring." Cara had suggested last night he might want a whole day to himself without her company, and, to her disappointment, he'd jumped at the suggestion. Pushing aside that thought, she sat beside her grandmother. "Nonna, you must be having a good day."

"I went to church this morning and took communion," Sophia said, her expression serene.

"She wouldn't even let us push her to a pew in her wheelchair," Rose put in. "Would you, Mamma? You got up and walked on your own two feet."

"I need to build up my strength for Cara's wedding."

Basil joined in the conversation without unlocking his gaze from the TV. "Your grandma gets any spryer, she'll be doing a jig at your reception." He groaned loudly in response to a fumble that gave the football to the Saints' opponent. "Just give the game away, why don't you, you fumble bums?"

Rose perched her reading glasses back on her nose

and read out a clue, "What's a four-letter word for wing? I should know that. I've run across it often enough."

Sophia resumed her crocheting, her fine stainless steel needle flashing.

Cara's spirits lifted, and her heart felt lighter at the seeming normalcy of this Sunday afternoon. Then she looked closer at what her grandmother was creating out of fine white thread. A tiny bootie.

A present for Frankie and Carmen's unborn baby, Cara deduced, her mood taking another dive downward into despondency.

Not only did she yearn to be Neil's wife. She yearned to be the mother of his child. But unless he changed his mindset, she would never realize either longing.

After last night's soul-bearing conversation following the lingerie episode, Cara's hopes were flagging.

Rose and Sophia both picked up on the fact Cara was feeling down in the dumps and cheerfully diagnosed her condition as bride's nerves. "We won't talk about the wedding," they declared, but the talk among the women soon centered around that very subject.

Cara put aside any private remorse, her perspective clear again. This wedding wasn't for her. It wasn't for Neil. It was for Sophia. And despite the emotional complications Cara hadn't foreseen, she didn't have a single regret over making her grandmother's final months on earth happy.

Whatever the price tag in later regrets, Cara would pay it without complaint.

Chapter Seven

Neil was at least thankful for the absence of any sense of déjù vu on the day of the wedding. There were too few parallels. He'd married Lisa in September, not June. The wedding guests on the bride's side had consisted mostly of friends and business associates of his in-laws rather than family members since Lisa was an only child of parents with no siblings.

The reception had taken place at an exclusive country club, not a rented hall, and a chamber music trio had played tasteful selections, whereas Cara had bowed to family pressure and hired a popular local band. Instead of a formal, sit-down dinner, food in ample quantities would be served in a buffet line. There was little doubt that the wedding guests today would probably have more fun than those wedding guests in Memphis had had at the more sedate reception.

The biggest difference was in Neil's state of mind on that previous wedding day eight years ago and his state of mind today. The twenty-six-year-old man, full of optimism about his future role as husband, had been eager to see his lovely bride walk down the aisle in her bridal finery. He'd looked forward to the upcoming honeymoon.

The thirty-four-year-old Neil had psyched himself up to speak his lines and act out his part and not reveal he was a phony. He felt nothing but dread when he thought about the wedding and the reception, but most of all he dreaded the compulsory honeymoon. The cabin at Lake Guntersville, Alabama, provided for separate sleeping quarters, but Neil didn't expect to sleep very much and not for the reason most bridegrooms failed to get their rest. It would be torture to avoid the intimacy that was against the rules he'd established.

All his emotions weren't negative, though, as he stood at the front of the church, and Cara appeared with her father. Pride and adoration swelled his chest and brought a natural smile to his lips as he gazed at her. She looked incredibly lovely in her ankle-length white satin dress, selected, he knew, over opposition from the female contingency in her family, some of whom had petitioned for a mile-long train and a full-length veil. Instead of the latter, she'd opted for a short

veil attached to a pearl tiara whose sheen comple-
mented her glossy black curls.

Hairstyle had generated another controversy, which
Neil hadn't intentionally gotten involved in, but Cara
had questioned him about his opinion. He'd answered
honestly that he liked her usual hairstyle a lot. The
fact that she hadn't changed it pleased him immensely.

Her bridal bouquet of yellow rosebuds and baby's
breath had been a sentimental choice. Yellow roses
were Sophia's favorite flower. Neil was the only person in the church privy to Cara's plan to deviate from
the standard wedding processional. Even her father
looked startled when she paused beside the pew where
Sophia sat, dabbing tears with a handkerchief. Smiling
at her grandmother, Cara broke off a rosebud, kissed
it and gave it to Sophia. Neil's throat tightened with
his own emotion as he, as no other onlooker could,
supplied the caption to Cara's loving act: This wedding is my gift to you, Nonna, she was saying.

Tears shimmered in Cara's beautiful brown eyes as
she gazed into Neil's eyes while she walked toward
him. He read her moment's uncertainty, her moment's
panic. The full realization of what she was about to
do must be dawning on her, he thought. Before now
she'd convinced herself that God would condone her
speaking wedding vows with the intention of breaking
them since He knew her heart. Now she was struck
by doubt at the very last second.

Neil put aside his own guilt and inner conflict in his
urge to lend her support. He smiled encouragement

and sent the silent message: Everything's okay. Don't be scared. We can accomplish this good deed together, you and I.

It was a good deed as far as motives went. He firmly believed that.

Cara smiled back, a tremulous smile that grew in brilliance as the crisis of doubt passed. She telegraphed her heartfelt gratitude: I can never thank you enough. There was more to the message, he knew, including an unconditional promise to repay him somehow, in any way he chose.

Neil didn't want payment. All he wanted was Cara's help in keeping their close bond intact during this temporary marriage. He needed her in his life, but as a sister/friend/employee, not a wife/lover/soulmate, whose loss would be the end of Neil. He couldn't survive that kind of tragedy twice.

He just couldn't.

Basil LaCroix kissed his youngest daughter on the cheek and delivered her to Neil. Neil clasped her hand and squeezed it. "You look so handsome, like my Prince Charming," Cara whispered. "And you look beautiful," he whispered back. Beautiful and alluring, her skin as creamy as the white satin bodice of her gown, which molded her ripe breasts and small waist. Unsettled by his surge of male possessiveness, Neil sucked in a deep breath and drew into his lungs the sweet scent of her bouquet blended with her perfume. The effect on him was more intoxicating than soothing.

The solemnity of the traditional marriage ceremony restored calm, but Neil couldn't manage to detach himself, not with Cara's hand clinging to his and transmitting tremors of her emotion. They spoke their vows. Neil's voice resonated with a grave seriousness over which he had no control. The sweetness and sincerity of Cara's voice pierced his heart like an arrow.

They'd needed to be convincing, but they hadn't needed to strike a note so true, so genuine. So binding.

Father Kerby pronounced them man and wife and gave Neil permission to kiss his bride. Cara lifted her face, and he bent and touched his lips to hers, the contact reverent and tender. Suddenly and totally unexpectedly, Cara's arms went up around his neck and she pulled his head down, crushing his mouth against her soft, voluptuous mouth. Neil couldn't help himself He kissed her the way he hadn't let himself kiss her all these hellish weeks, with hunger and passion, even mating briefly with her tongue.

Delighted titters and guffaws and a spattering of applause brought him to his senses. Still, stopping the kiss took enormous willpower. He wanted to go on kissing Cara, audience or no audience.

Because this *had* to be his one and only lapse. His one and only taste of the sheer heaven of being her lover.

Cara looked dazed as she opened her eyes and reluctantly withdrew her arms. They made their exit march down the aisle. Outside the church, a limousine waited to transport bride and groom to the reception hall. In a shower of rice, Neil helped Cara into the back seat.

She still had that dazed look. "I hope you're not mad at me," she said, sounding dazed, too.

"Mad at you?"

"Making you kiss me, like that. It wasn't something I planned. I just acted on impulse."

She turned toward him, lifting both hands. Neil's heart leaped as he guessed her intention, to instigate another passionate kiss. He shrank back. "Don't," he said, his voice coming out harsh.

"You have rice in your hair," she explained, her expression hurt.

Neil brushed his hand over his head roughly, dislodging the white grains.

"I'm sorry," she said, blinking hard, obviously on the brink of tears. "I wish..." She didn't complete her thought.

"For goodness sake, don't cry."

"I won't."

"I'm not angry. Not at you. Okay?" He gently brushed white grains from her hair. Despite his turmoil, he enjoyed touching the lustrous black curls. Heaven help him, he could have enjoyed stealing kisses on the ride, enjoyed acting like a real bridegroom if only the sick fear in the pit of his stomach didn't prevent him. "We'll be there soon. How about a happy smile?" he coaxed. "Come on. Remember, we're doing this for Sophia."

The reminder worked. "For a moment I forgot all

about Nonna and got wrapped up in myself,'' she confided, wrinkling her nose adorably. ''Did you see her face in the church, Neil? Her expression made the whole thing worthwhile for me. The pretence, the guilty conscience.''

''I've never seen a human being that transported with joy,'' Neil said sincerely. ''I was almost afraid she would sprout wings and fly off to Heaven, then and there.''

''Thank you for the millionth time.'' She framed his face and kissed him on the cheek.

Neil gave her a brotherly hug, and the old status quo was restored, much to his relief.

''Congratulations, son.'' Dean Griffin, an older version of Neil himself, offered his hand in a hearty handshake, simultaneously clapping Neil on the shoulder.

''Your father and I couldn't be happier over having Cara as a daughter-in-law.'' Judith Griffin, petite in her mother-of-the-groom green silk dress, rose on tiptoes to hug Neil around the neck with tanned arms. ''You have to promise that you and Cara will come to Florida and visit us on your first vacation.''

Neil had a fleeting vision of himself and Cara on a white-sand beach and quickly banished the picture of her in a bikini. It speeded up his pulse and deepened his guilt. He made some non-committal answer, trying his best to act the role of the happy bridegroom. Damn, this was worse than he'd expected, getting through the reception. He felt awful knowing he was deceiving his parents.

Accepting the good wishes from the big LaCroix clan wasn't any easier. It made matters worse that every single one of Cara's sisters and brothers, all of whom he knew from growing up in the same neighborhood, seemed to be entirely in favor of the marriage that they didn't have a clue was fake.

Neil escaped onto the dance floor with Cara and soon discovered he hadn't really gained a respite for himself. Instead he'd ventured into new, even worse torments.

"Not like that, Neil," Cara whispered when he'd put his arm around her waist, clasped her hand and guided her a few steps in time to the slow music.

"Did I step on your feet?" he asked, slightly befuddled.

"No, but everyone's watching us."

"So?" Neil wasn't Fred Astaire, but he wasn't a bad dancer either.

"Silly, you can't hold me like I was your maiden aunt. We have to act like a new bride and groom about to go off on a honeymoon." Cara snuggled closer, giving him little choice but to tighten his arm.

"Hey, that's more like it!" called Tony LaCroix from the sidelines, and there were other similar responses. The party had already begun.

Neil flashed a weak grin, trying desperately to hang on to the awareness of onlookers and not drown in the drugged pleasure of moving his body to the music and feeling Cara's body movements become one with his. She sighed and snuggled closer, murmuring, "You're such a good dancer."

"So are you." Conversation seemed to be his best bet. "We've had a little practice dancing together through the years, haven't we? Remember your sister Natalie's wedding reception? What was that—twenty years ago? You must have been about nine. I was about fourteen." Neil dredged up a memory of her in a blue velvet dress.

"I kept pulling you out on the dance floor," she recalled. "You were so sweet to put up with me. I had such a crush on you." She slid her hand along his shoulder in a caressing motion that sent heat over his skin under the layers of clothing. "I seem to have had a crush on you my whole life. The truth is I always intended to marry you someday."

"Now you tell me. I think I've been had."

The slow number the band was playing was almost over, thank goodness. Neil dispensed with reminiscence for the time being. He closed his eyes and immersed himself in the sheer heaven of dancing with the twenty-nine-year-old Cara, beautiful and sexy in her white satin wedding gown.

His bride. If only for a little while.

"Look at Rose dancing with that handsome husband of yours. Eight children, and she's still light on her feet."

It wasn't necessary to direct Cara's attention to the

dance floor. She'd been watching Neil and her mother, but, admittedly, her focus had been mainly on him. Gazing at him gave her such pleasure. He was so tall and good-looking in his tuxedo. To see him interact with everyone at the reception was to see proof of his likable personality, his courteous manners, his sense of humor. *My husband,* a little thrilled voice inside her kept saying.

"You're pretty light on your feet, too, Nonna," she remarked, holding up her end of the conversation. "I noticed that when you were dancing with Neil earlier."

"Such a charmer, he is. That smile of his warms the heart of even an old lady like me." She patted Cara's hand. "You should see your face light up when he smiles at you. It's a beautiful sight, two young people madly in love with each other."

How I wish, Cara thought. Neil loved her, a steady, supportive love, but he wasn't romantically in love with her and didn't want to be. Perhaps that could change if he would allow it to, but he was trying hard to keep their relationship the same as it always had been.

Out of fairness, Cara had to follow his lead even though she felt differently. She could probably rock the boat by seducing him against his will during their honeymoon. There would be opportunity with the two of them sharing the cabin in Alabama, and he *was* attracted to her physically. But she had no intention of trying to seduce him. When and if Neil ever became her lover, she wanted him to make that decision himself, willingly.

Sophia didn't notice Cara's wistful mood. The elderly woman rambled on happily, optimistic about her youngest granddaughter's future as Mrs. Neil Griffin.

Cara silently gave thanks that she'd been able to bring this happiness to her grandmother, who'd lavished so much love on her from the time Cara was born. Later on, Cara might pay a bigger price than she'd foreseen when she'd dreamed up the idea of a temporary marriage. That price might entail untold misery and disappointment. But now wasn't the time to worry about such a gloomy outcome. Especially when she was hopeful that Neil would come around and change his attitude. Hopeful that eventually she really would become his wife in the real sense of the word.

Become the mother of his children. What a thrilling thought that was!

"Those brothers of mine! They must have guessed we were going to ditch my car and drive your pickup to Alabama. So they decorated it, too!" Cara's voice was full of laughter as well as chagrin. A glance at Neil told her he was reacting good-naturedly, too, as they sat in his driveway, noting the Just Married announcements scrawled in white and almost covering the red paint of his pickup.

"Wait till I get my hands on Jimmy Boudreaux,"

he said, a grin tugging at the corners of his mouth. "I'll bet he let the cat out of the bag."

"You told Jimmy our plans? Why did you do that?"

"I asked him to pick up your car while we were gone and have it washed and waxed."

"How sweet."

"How stupid, as it turns out." He made a wry face. "Now we have our choice of which automobile to drive."

They decided to drive her sporty car.

"After I change out of this tuxedo, I'll get rid of the noisemakers," Neil said. A whole collection of cans and other metal objects had been attached to the bottom framework of her car and dragged against the pavement.

"I'll help you. I can scoot up under the car."

"No way," he scoffed. "I'm the mechanic."

They went inside his house and paused in the hallway outside his guest bedroom. She'd insisted on taking it for hers, refusing his repeated offers to let her move into the master bedroom. She figured she was disrupting his life enough, as it was.

"Could you unzip me, please?" she asked, turning her back to him. Several seconds passed before she finally felt his fingers attending to the task she hadn't meant to be unsettling for him. During the pause her heart had started beating faster with a ridiculous suspense.

It was so quiet in the house that the zipper sound seemed loud and abrasive.

"There," Neil said. His voice was taut.

"Thanks. I can handle the rest." She half-turned and smiled at him. He didn't smile back, and she noticed his expression showed strain. "Want me to undo your cuff links?"

"Please." He moved back a half step and extended his arms.

Cara had trouble and bent slightly forward as she worked at freeing his left cuff. Her wedding dress started to slide down, but she was wearing a strapless bra and didn't have to worry about exposing her breasts.

"Dammit, Cara!" he exclaimed, jerking his wrists away. "Your dress!"

"I almost had that cuff undone," she protested, grasping the bodice of the dress and tugging it back up.

"That's okay," he said in a strangled voice. "I'll manage."

"Neil—" She was talking to his back since he was striding toward his bedroom. "It's silly to get all upset over nothing!"

"Would you please just change your clothes so we can get out of here?"

Cara hesitated and then followed after him, propelled by an urgency to make things right between them, then and there. "I hope you don't think I was trying to be provocative by showing you a little cleavage. Because I wasn't. Honest.''

''I believe you. Okay?''

He was pulling savagely at his left cuff. The cuff link went flying, richocheted off the wall and dropped to the carpet. Cara stopped to pick it up. In the doorway of his bedroom, she stooped to pick up the other one. ''Neil, you're ruining that shirt!'' Buttons were popping. ''I've never seen you act like this!''

''Some privacy would be appreciated,'' he bit out, stripping off the shirt.

In the midst of her concern, Cara was admiring his bared upper torso. The sight brought back memories of him when he'd mowed his parents' lawn, shirtless, muscles playing smoothly under his tan. She opened her mouth to say something and then her mouth went dry as he dropped his trousers. He wore boxer shorts instead of briefs, but Cara could still see for herself that he was physically aroused—evidence that didn't exactly make her feel calm and collected. Knees suddenly weak, Cara leaned against the door facing.

''This isn't going to be easy keeping our relationship the same. Not at first, anyway,'' she said.

''No kidding.'' He'd sat down on the end of the bed and peeled off his socks. With elbows on knees, he dropped his head into his hands, a picture of a man wracked by problems.

Cara ached with the desire to go over to him, touch him, reassure him. But she burned with a different womanly desire that made it entirely unwise to take a step inside the room.

"Just give me fifteen minutes, and I'll be ready to go," she promised and sped back down the hallway to her bedroom, the cuff links cutting into her palm.

Neil had obviously changed into navy slacks and a crisp short-sleeved cotton shirt in record time because he'd already removed the tin cans and assortment of other dangling objects when Cara emerged from the house, wheeling her two suitcases. She glanced at the pile he'd assembled on the lawn and saw old aluminum pie plates and dented pot lids.

"Some of that stuff looks like it might have come from my old playhouse," she commented.

"I was thinking the same thing," Neil said. He was folding a tarp he'd evidently spread on the driveway to keep from soiling his clothes when he scooted up under the automobile. To her relief he seemed as relaxed as he'd been on their arrival earlier, prior to the tense scene she'd caused unintentionally by asking him to unzip her dress. He must have recovered from his frustrated state, Cara reflected, glad to postpone the apology she'd rehearsed.

"Remember when I used to make mud pies garnished with leaves and flowers and serve them to you?" she asked. Her brothers would never take the time to humor her, but Neil had usually spared her at least a few minutes to play Let's Pretend. Was it any wonder she'd grown up adoring him?

He nodded to indicate he did remember. His smile was reminiscent. "You wore that cute little apron."

"Nonna made it for me. I still have it, packed away with favorite toys in my parents' attic. I always figured that someday—" Cara didn't complete the sentence when she realized what she'd been about to say in a wistful tone of voice.

Neil had filled in the blanks for himself, she could tell from his expression. "You always figured that someday your little girl would wear it when she made mud pies," he stated.

"Silly, huh? If I ever had a daughter, she might be a tomboy and not the type to play house anyway." She shrugged and pulled the two suitcases to the open trunk.

"Don't lift those," he said. "I'll get them."

"Okay."

The conversation had left Cara with an empty, sad feeling, but she tried her best to act as if nothing were wrong. While he stowed the luggage, she deposited the pile of junk in a bin for recyclables in the garage.

Not surprisingly, her efforts at cheerfulness didn't fool Neil. She was aware of his concerned glances. Then when they were on the highway, headed toward Alabama, he said, "You're only twenty-nine, Cara. That's much too young to worry about a biological clock ticking away your childbearing years. These days some career women put off having a family until they're in their forties."

"I know."

"Don't even think about giving that little apron to one of your nieces. You'll have a daughter someday." He squeezed her hand.

"How on earth did you guess that I *have* considered giving it to a niece?" Cara asked in amazement. "Are you a mind reader?"

"I know how your mind works when it comes to your family."

A tender impulse took hold, and she raised his hand to her lips and kissed his knuckles. Immediately he pulled his hand away and rubbed his knuckles hard against his thigh as though to erase the imprint of her lips.

"For goodness sake, Neil! I was only being affectionate. I wasn't trying to—to arouse you," Cara protested, both hurt and indignant over his response. "It's confusing. One moment we're old buddies and the next moment you overreact to some perfectly innocent action on my part."

"I'm sorry. Believe me, I would control myself better if I could." He'd returned his hand to the wheel and was gripping it hard. "This is my problem, not yours."

"Of course, it's my problem, too. I want us to have fun on this trip, not be on pins and needles." She gathered her courage. "Forgive me if I'm being too personal, but you mentioned once that you hadn't had sex during the last three years. That's a long time for a man to be celibate, isn't it?"

"It's not a record by any means."

"But haven't you gotten—" Cara couldn't think of a ladylike word. "Haven't you gotten horny?"

"This is a hell of a discussion." A grin tugged at the corners of Neil's mouth.

"My whole point is that nature is taking its course."

"Well, nature isn't going to win out on this trip. For one thing, I didn't come prepared. Did you?"

Cara felt herself blushing because she'd actually deliberated over whether to buy condoms and had been tempted to do so. "No, I didn't."

"And you're not on the Pill, are you?"

She answered negatively again.

It was apparent that in his view, enough had been said on the subject of sex and the lack thereof during their fake honeymoon. "How about some music?" he suggested.

Cara selected a country and western CD she knew was one of his favorites and played it. She would have liked to know if she and only she had roused Neil's slumbering sex drive during the past three years since he'd been widowed. But what good would that knowledge do her? She wouldn't act on it and try to lure him into being her lover, with or without birth control.

"Do we have time to ride along the beach?" asked Cara when they passed the Mississippi Welcome Rest Stop.

"Sure. There's no hurry to get to Mobile. We have a confirmed reservation at the hotel." They were staying overnight in Mobile and driving to Guntersville the next day.

He took a beach exit off I-10, and fifteen minutes later they were cruising along the Mississippi Gulf Coast on Highway 90, enjoying the view of white sand and open sea on their right-hand side and admiring elegant old homes on their left-hand side. Interspersed with picturesque marinas featuring shrimp boats were the more numerous floating casinos, some of them garish palaces sitting on barges. Others were converted seagoing vessels.

"Want to stop at a casino and try your luck?" asked Neil. Dawdling and arriving late in Mobile seemed like a wise idea. The more tired he was when they checked into the hotel, the better his chances of getting some rest on this, the first night of their honeymoon.

Cara jumped at his suggestion. "Let's do stop! I'd love to see that new casino in Biloxi that I heard about on the news. It's supposed to be straight out of Las Vegas with designer shops and a fancy lobby."

"We'll stop there then and arrange to send the car out to have it washed."

"You mean you don't enjoy all this attention?" she teased. "People waving and blowing their horns?"

"I guess I wasn't cut out for celebrity."

"You're more the undercover-agent type."

"More the solid citizen, business-owner, average-guy type."

"Average? Never," she declared. "You've always been my hero."

"I'm no hero," he said.

"By my definition, you are. You've come to my rescue often enough."

Neil turned his head to look at her just as she leaned over toward him. She'd meant to kiss him on the cheek, he realized. Instead she kissed him lightly on the lips. Immediately a horn blared out behind them. The automobile passed, arms waving out the windows and teenagers' faces wreathed in grins.

Neil let the hero issue drop. They'd just been engaging in banter anyway, not a serious discussion. He certainly didn't see himself as possessing heroic qualities like great courage and daring. He was simply a man, all too human, all too scarred by his experiences.

Once he'd embraced the philosophy of if you fall off the horse, climb back on and ride; don't let anything get the best of you. That was before his small family had been wiped out in a few seconds, and climbing back on the horse amounted to remarrying and risking the same emotional devastation again.

Call him a coward, but Neil wouldn't—*couldn't*—leave himself open to be blindsided in the same way. If he had any doubts, all he had to do was visualize a certain cemetery in Tennessee.

"Wow. I'm impressed," Cara said.

"Me, too."

Hand in hand, they stood in the casino hotel lobby, admiring the marble floor, the grand windows and oversize doors, the high quality of workmanship evident in the varnished woodwork. Live trees and land-scaping added to the ambience.

"The owners sure didn't spare any expense in designing and building this permanent structure," Neil observed.

"Just the casino itself floats on the water?"

"Right. We should be able to detect the transition."

"I wonder how they keep the two parts level, the land part and the floating part."

"Probably by some means of making the barge sections lighter or heavier as the water rises and falls."

"Personally, I thought it was a smart move by the Mississippi legislature to require all casinos to be floating structures as a safeguard against a lot of white-elephant buildings someday if gambling runs its course and casinos go out of business here on the Gulf Coast."

"I thought so, too," he said.

They strolled along the shopping arcade, pausing at shop windows to gaze at upscale merchandise in artistic displays.

"Almost makes you wish you were rich and could buy all this pricey designer stuff," Cara remarked.

He squeezed her hand, and his tone was indulgent as he replied, "We're not rich, but we're not exactly poor either. If you see something you want, we could probably spring for it."

"I don't see anything I need." His use of *we,* as though they were a real married couple with combined finances, made it easy to imagine she had everything in the world to make her happy.

Was he already changing his attitude about theirs being a temporary marriage? Cara knew she shouldn't get her hopes too high this soon.

"According to Allison, this arcade is on a par with those on the strip in Las Vegas," she remarked.

"Close maybe, but on a par? I don't know if I'd go that far, having seen the shopping arcade at Caesar's Palace."

"I didn't realize you'd been to Las Vegas."

"Once. Lisa and I went with her mother and dad. They go often. He's a big enough gambler that they get comped rooms at Caesar's Palace."

Cara was mentally kicking herself for introducing Lisa into the conversation, however innocently. She knew that Neil's memories of his deceased wife usually brought the grief back. Surprisingly, he'd spoken Lisa's name easily and his recollection of the trip to Las Vegas hadn't seemed to trigger pain. Was he healing?

"You keep in touch with them?" she asked.

"We call each other now and then. They're nice people and treated me really well. Here's the entrance to the casino. Let's go feed some coins into the slots."

"Maybe we'll hit a big jackpot like a co-worker of Tony's did. He won $10,000."

They entered the colorful, noisy world of flashing lights and electronic jingling. Another couple passed them, walking faster as though in more of a hurry to begin their gaming entertainment. "I feel lucky!" the woman said.

Cara smiled to herself, thinking to herself that she felt awfully lucky at that moment, too, and winning or not winning a jackpot had little to do with her mood. She could be anywhere and feel lucky, holding Neil's hand, looking forward to days in his company.

And maybe she'd even get lucky enough to have a real honeymoon!

Chapter Eight

"I made the reservation two weeks ago. Here's the confirmation number." Neil tapped the piece of paper he'd laid on the counter.

The front-desk clerk, a prematurely balding young man, kept punching buttons on his keyboard and shaking his head in consternation. "I'm awfully sorry for the mix-up, sir. But we just don't have two adjoining rooms for tonight that are vacant. The best I can do, I'm afraid, is give you two rooms on separate floors."

"That won't do," Neil said without even considering the option. Even though this trip wasn't a bon-afide honeymoon, it just didn't seem right to stick Cara in a room by herself off on another floor. "What about a suite?"

More punching of keys. More head-shaking. Then the clerk started nodding. "I have a deluxe one-bedroom suite that's unoccupied."

"With a full-size sofa?"

"All our deluxe suites have full-size sofas."

"I'll take it." Was it Neil's imagination or did Cara quietly exhale a sigh of relief?

In the elevator, she said, "I'll sleep on the sofa. You take the bed. You're taller."

"I'm sleeping on the sofa," Neil stated. "This is my fault. I should have called yesterday and double-checked on the accommodations for tonight."

"You had good reason to expect that a big hotel chain could keep things straight."

She entered the suite ahead of him and declared, "How nice! Our own cozy living room. And I love the color scheme. Green and peach. Look, we have a wet bar."

Earlier she'd gotten drowsy in the car, but now she sounded wide awake, Neil noticed. So was he. "Good. I'm thirsty."

Cara checked out the contents of the small refrigerator. "Wine, beer, colas. And miniature bottles of hard stuff, if you want a cocktail."

"I believe I'd like a beer."

"Me, too. Turn on the TV, why don't you?" she suggested, taking out two bottles of imported beer.

They both kicked off their shoes and made themselves comfortable on the sofa. Neil followed her example and propped his feet on the coffee table. Using the remote, he flipped around and found a late-night show.

Cara sipped her beer and seemed to be enjoying the chitchat between the host and his guest, a professional skater who'd been barred from competition and recently reinstated. During a commercial, Cara sighed contentedly and rolled her head sideways to smile at him. "I had a lot of fun today, in spite of everything. I hope you did, too."

Neil wanted so badly to express affection, take her hand, give her a hug, kiss her on the cheek, but he just didn't trust himself to make physical contact. "Sure, I had fun."

"You're not just saying that to humor me?"

"I'm not. Oh, there were definitely some bad moments mixed in, too. But the good outweighed the bad."

"I'm glad."

He could sense she needed more reassurance. "Not once did I think, 'I'm sorry I agreed to this.'"

"Thank you for telling me that." She reached for his hand and squeezed it. They linked fingers together on the sofa cushion between them. Neil still had to battle the need to be more demonstrative.

The late show went off. "Another beer?" Cara asked.

"No, thanks. I'm about ready to call it a night, if you are."

"I am. Please let me take the sofa. It may be 'full-size,' but it's not long enough for you to stretch out. You're over six feet tall.''

She had a legitimate point. ''I'd rather be uncomfortable than know you were uncomfortable.''

''I promise you I won't be.''

Neil reluctantly gave in.'

Housekeeping had delivered extra bedding. Cara set about at once spreading a sheet on the sofa as though wanting to claim her spot before he changed his mind. Neil carried one of his suitcases into the bedroom and felt worse at the sight of a king-size bed. Briefly he considered an alternate plan. Why couldn't both of them sleep in the bed? The reaction of his body gave him the answer, loud and clear. *No way.* Her presence in the next room was going to pose a big enough obstacle to relaxation.

Neil dug out one of the two pairs of pajamas he'd bought especially for this trip. He smiled without humor at the notion of a bridegroom buying pajamas for his honeymoon. A male version of a chastity belt? he asked himself with irony as he shook out the bottoms. Before stepping into them, he deliberated about whether to leave his boxer shorts on or take them off. Take them off, Neil decided. The air touching his naked body when he shucked his underwear seemed to have an arousing effect. Quickly he donned the pajamas, bottoms and top.

He'd brought along a bathrobe, too, but left it in the suitcase. Putting it on seemed pretty silly.

After a quick trip to the bathroom, he went to the

door of the living room to announce, "The bathroom's all yours now."

"Okay, thanks." Cara was kneeling on the carpet in front of an open suitcase. She rose to her feet as she glanced at him. Her smile changed as she took in his appearance with surprise and female interest. "Do you normally sleep in pajamas?"

"No."

"So you bought some especially for our—this trip?"

"I didn't own any old ones." Neil was trying not to look at the silky yellow garments she held, one in each hand. Presumably a night gown and a robe of the same flimsy material. The color was familiar, bringing back that disturbing scene outside her town house when he'd met her coming home from the lingerie shower.

"You didn't have to go out and buy pajamas." Cara's fascinated gaze was making Neil sorry he hadn't put on the bathrobe. He managed not to glance down at his crotch, which had to be noticeable. The stimulation was definitely getting to him. "Those are nice, though," she was saying, walking over to him. "Kind of like a lightweight sweat suit."

It took all Neil's willpower not to flinch as she fingered the cotton knit. Heat shimmered over his skin and his breathing became shallow and quick. "Well, I'll say good-night," he said.

"Good night." She sounded breathless, too.

Neil bent to kiss her on the cheek just as she rose

on tiptoes, apparently meaning to kiss him on the cheek. Somehow they ended up with faces an inch apart. Her pretty brown eyes widened as though she were caught up in a trance and her full, soft lips parted in invitation. Frozen in place, Neil fought the fog of desire that clouded his brain. His muscles trembled with the exertion of trying to regain control of his body and straighten up, move away out of the danger zone. He didn't *want* to move away from her...

Finally Cara saved him. Saved them both. She closed her eyes and broke the spell. "Sleep tight," she whispered and gave him a sweet peck on the cheek.

"You, too." Neil retreated into the bedroom, climbed into the huge bed and jerked the cover up to his armpits. Tomorrow he would look back and be thankful he'd gotten through this first hellish night without compromising their marriage agreement, but that knowledge didn't do anything to ease the frustration.

Or the yearning that went beyond physical need.

Cara hadn't followed behind him immediately, but soon she entered the bedroom, on her way to the bathroom. "I'll try to be as quiet as a mouse and not wake you in case you fall asleep right away," she said in a lowered voice as though he may already be drifting off.

"Don't worry. I sleep like a rock," Neil answered.

"I'm still not very sleepy, but maybe a long soak in the tub will help."

It won't help me a bit, Neil thought, mentally groaning. Aloud he said, "Hope it does the trick."

After the door closed behind her, he got up and found a car magazine he'd stuck in his suitcase for just such an emergency as this. Back in bed again with the lamp turned on, he thumbed through and located an interesting article. He began to read, doing his best to close out sounds of water running and block out images of Cara removing her clothes.

Neil had almost succeeded in concentrating on the words on the page when the running water stopped. Now the challenge was not to imagine her stepping into the oversize tub, naked. In desperation, he mumbled a sentence aloud. Its meaning still didn't sink in. Neil tossed the magazine aside in defeat and threw back the sheet.

With his robe tightly belted around his waist, he abandoned the bedroom for the time being. But out in the living room, Cara's open suitcase immediately drew his gaze. He muttered a despairing curse. Evidently she'd selected underwear to wear tomorrow. Neatly arranged in full view were a white bra and white bikini panties, confections of lace and silk.

All day tomorrow he would have to try not to think about her wearing the sexy bra and panties underneath her clothes. "This is worse than I expected," Neil murmured under his breath, turning his back on the suitcase and heading over to the wet bar. After surveying the contents of the refrigerator, he opened another beer. The hard liquor in the miniature bottles were higher in alcohol content, he knew, but Neil wasn't much of a drinker and hadn't become one even in the worst stages of his grief.

With the couch converted into Cara's makeshift bed, he felt too much like an intruder to sit on one of the easy chairs. Instead, Neil stood in front of the TV while he drank his beer, remote control in his free hand, flipping through the channels. He'd lowered the volume almost to the mute level.

Cara hadn't emerged from the bathroom as he took his last swallow. Reflecting that he would do well to avoid encountering her out here, Neil disposed of the empty beer bottle and went back to bed. Not long after he'd doused the lamp, the bathroom door eased open.

Don't look, he ordered himself, but he looked anyway and was treated—and tortured—with the view of her womanly form silhouetted against the rectangle of dim light, her night garments as filmy and diaphanous as wreaths of clouds around the moon. Within seconds she'd reached and turned off the bathroom light, but a few seconds were long enough to etch on the screen of his mind the lovely sight he'd seen.

"Are you asleep, Neil?" she asked, her voice barely audible.

"No, but I'm getting there," he lied, trying to sound drowsy.

"I hope I didn't disturb you."

"No, you didn't."

"Good. See you in the morning."

Neil didn't know whether he heard the whisper of

silk and lace or imagined it as she exited the bedroom, her footsteps soundless on the carpet. There was no doubt that the scent of sweet, clean woman filled his lungs and made him light-headed. Briefly she appeared in the living-room door, a vision of alluring femininity. Then she was gone, leaving him to cope with an aroused body and a soul plagued with yearning.

What about her dissatisfaction? Her yearning? Neil felt rotten on Cara's behalf that she was spending her wedding night on a damn sofa in a hotel.

Cara was wide awake after lying there for what seemed like an hour, changing positions every few minutes. Maybe if she watched TV without the volume turned on, that would help her get sleepy, she reflected. But the flickering light might disturb Neil. She'd left the door open between the living room and bedroom.

The obvious solution was to get up and close it.

In the darkness she rose and tiptoed across the carpet, feeling her way slowly so as not to stumble into furniture or trip over suitcases. With her mission accomplished she felt her way back to an end table without mishap and turned on a lamp. The TV remote seemed to be missing. She was certain Neil had laid it on the coffee table.

After a search Cara eventually spotted the gadget over on a shelf of the cabinet that housed the TV itself. How had it gotten there? she wondered. A minute or so later she answered her own question when she was getting herself a soft drink at the wet bar. There were three empty beer bottles, not two, in the trash can.

Neil must have come out here and helped himself to another beer and watched TV while she was bathing. Cara imagined him doing those things and went weak in the knees, just like she had when she'd looked up earlier and seen him wearing his teal knit pajamas. He'd looked so masculine and sexy, the bottoms molding his crotch and his thighs.

My husband, the hunk, Cara thought wistfully, popping the top on her can of soda. She winced at the loud sound and looked over at the bedroom door, heart drumming at the possibility she'd awakened him and he would get up to check on her, blinking sleepily, his hair tousled.

Apparently she hadn't wakened him.

Darn.

Cara sipped her soft drink and fantasized. In one scenario she slipped into the bedroom and got in bed with Neil. He pulled her into his arms, all his doubts vanishing. In another scenario he came out and collected her from the sofa, picking her up and carrying her to bed with him. Cara closed her eyes and moaned with the ecstasy of his intimate caresses and kisses, her intimate caresses and kisses...

She stopped herself. None of what she was imagining was going to happen tonight. It might not happen tomorrow night, and she had to be patient.

Had to.

And hope she didn't die of longing before they became lovers.

Bleary-eyed, Neil raised his arm and peered at his watch. Six o'clock. Too early to get up, especially since he hadn't fallen asleep until after 3:00 a.m. when he'd shed the damn pajama bottoms. An hour before that he'd peeled off the top.

Go back to sleep, Neil ordered himself and closed his eyes. It was no use, though. He was groggy and tired, but awake.

Buck naked, he headed for the bathroom. Modesty didn't seem much of a priority since Cara was undoubtedly still sleeping. And in his dragged-out condition, a fig leaf would do fine to cover him. There was something to be said for fatigue in combating lust, Neil reflected, yawning.

A shower and a shave revived him to the extent that he wrapped a towel around his hips before he reentered the bedroom. A fig leaf wasn't seeming quite so substantial a covering. The door to the living room was still closed and stayed closed while he got fully dressed except for his shoes, which he remembered kicking under the coffee table.

Quietly he opened the door into the outer room. No movement. No sense that Cara was awake. The front of the sofa wasn't visible yet. Neil walked in his sock feet, skirting the nearer end of the sofa. He was braced for the sight of her and expected her to look adorable

An Important Message from the Editors

Dear Reader,

Because you've chosen to read one of our fine romance novels, we'd like to say "thank you!" And, as a <u>special</u> way to thank you, we've selected <u>two more</u> of the books you love so well, <u>plus</u> an exciting mystery gift, to send you absolutely **FREE**!

Please enjoy them with our compliments...

Rebecca Pearson

Editor

P.S. And because we <u>value</u> our customers, we've attached something extra inside...

EDITOR'S
FREE GIFT
SEAL
THANK YOU

Peel off seal and Place inside...

How to validate your
Editor's FREE GIFT "Thank You"

1. Peel off gift seal from front cover. Place it in space provided at right. This automatically entitles you to receive 2 FREE BOOKS and a fabulous mystery gift.

2. Send back this card and you'll get 2 brand-new Silhouette Special Edition® novels. These books have a cover price of $4.50 each in the U.S. and $5.25 each in Canada, but they are yours to keep absolutely free.

3. There's no catch. You're under no obligation to buy anything. We charge nothing—ZERO—for your first shipment. And you don't have to make any minimum number of purchases—not even one!

4. The fact is, thousands of readers enjoy receiving their books by mail from the Silhouette Reader Service™. They enjoy the convenience of home delivery...they like getting the best new novels at discount prices BEFORE they're available in stores...and they love their *Heart to Heart* subscriber newsletter featuring author news, horoscopes, recipes, book reviews and much more!

5. We hope that after receiving your free books you'll want to remain a subscriber. But the choice is yours— to continue or cancel, any time at all! So why not take us up on our invitation, with no risk of any kind. You'll be glad you did!

6. Don't forget to detach your FREE BOOKMARK. And remember...just for validating your Editor's Free Gift Offer, we'll send you THREE gifts, *ABSOLUTELY FREE!*

GET A FREE MYSTERY GIFT...

YOURS FREE!

SURPRISE MYSTERY GIFT COULD BE YOURS _FREE_ AS A SPECIAL "THANK YOU" FROM THE EDITORS OF SILHOUETTE

Visit us online at
www.eHarlequin.com

and sweet, probably curled up in the fetal position and covered with a sheet. Definitely covered with a sheet.

Neil stopped dead in his tracks and gazed hard in shock. No fetal position. No sheet. Cara was lying on her stomach, one hand tucked under her hip. Her nightgown was twisted and hiked up nearly to her waist, exposing a bare rounded bottom. Neil cursed silently and got down on his knees to retrieve his shoes.

Flooded by regret and apology—not to mention hotly aroused, Neil didn't dare hang around long enough to put on his shoes. He waited until he was out in the corridor.

Down in the coffee shop he ordered coffee he no longer needed to bring him fully awake. He probably needed a tranquilizer more than caffeine

"That was sweet of you to wait and have breakfast with me," Cara said, buttering a flaky hot biscuit. She smiled at Neil, who was pouring syrup on his pancakes.

"It wasn't a problem to wait. I wasn't hungry."

"You were supposed to say, 'It was worth the wait just to sit across the table from you, my darling wife.'"

He scowled in response to her teasing. "Is it starting already? Nag, nag, nag."

Cara laughed, highly amused. "For a second there, you really had me thinking you were serious."

"I am serious." He grinned at her, and her spirits soared.

Things were going to work out eventually. She was sure of it.

After breakfast, they set out on the second leg of their trip to northern Alabama, with Cara behind the wheel. "Feel free to catch a few zzz's," she told Neil. "After all, you only got three hours sleep last night. I got almost six hours." She'd dropped off to sleep around two in the morning and hadn't awakened until eight.

"I feel pretty alert," he replied. "And being sleep-deprived might work in my favor tonight."

"I hope you didn't lie awake feeling guilty because I was on the sofa."

"That was only part of the problem."

"It felt odd wearing pajamas?"

"Extremely."

"You should have taken them off."

"I did. Finally."

"Oh. Good." Cara's pulse rate had picked up. She was thinking that she would have had even more trouble falling asleep herself if she'd been visualizing him lying in bed and *not* wearing the clingy knit pajamas. "D you ordinarily—" She broke off, realizing she would probably be better off not knowing for sure he slept nude. "I'm being too personal."

"Usually I sleep in my boxer shorts," he said, answering the question she hadn't finished asking. "I got in the habit when I was traveling a lot with my sales rep job and staying in hotels. A couple of times emergency alarms went off in the middle of the night. I got a little paranoid about the idea of being awakened without a stitch on.''

''I don't blame you.'' Cara glanced over at him during a brief silence. ''What?'' she asked, sensing he had something on his mind.

He still didn't speak right away, causing her to become more curious. And, for some reason, nervous. ''This morning you were lying on your stomach,'' he said.

''Was I? I was lying on my side when I woke up.'' Cara dimly remembered rousing up and pulling up the sheet during the early morning hours. Daylight had seeped into the room. Was that before or after he'd passed through and seen her? Before, she hoped, because her gown had been hiked up. He would have gotten quite a view, an embarrassing thought.

''So you sleep on your stomach?'' he persisted.

''And on my back and on both sides. I flop around. And I usually kick off the cover,'' she added, sneaking a quick look at him.

''Yes, you do.''

She blushed. ''At least I was fairly modest, on my stomach. Except now you know where I carry around my extra pounds.''

''What I saw didn't need any improvement,'' Neil said.

''Is it any wonder I'm crazy about you?'' Cara said

lightly. "You always made me feel I was just about perfect the way I was."

"You are just about perfect as far as I'm concerned."

His tone was light, too, but sincere. As flattering as his words were, she couldn't help wishing she was his ideal woman for a wife, instead of a younger sister. Then maybe he would have stuck around this morning instead of going down to the coffee shop and not returning until she was up and dressed.

Sure, Cara understood Neil's unwillingness to expose himself to tragedy again, but at the same time she felt a sense of rejection. He loved her, cared about her, but not the way she yearned for him to love her. And it wasn't just marital sex she wanted so badly. It was marital *intimacy*. Removing the barriers, sharing everything, becoming a *couple*.

Patient. You have to be patient, Cara reminded herself.

Chapter Nine

"I love this hilly country, don't you? This highway's like a roller coaster!"

Neil smiled and nodded. He was enjoying Cara's enthusiasm and zest for life as much as he was enjoying the scenery. "You and I can appreciate these Alabama hills, coming from southern Louisiana, where it's so flat. Maybe another year—" He broke off, realizing he'd been on the verge of mapping out travel plans for future years. Years when they wouldn't be taking vacations together.

Cara looked over at him, but she didn't press him to finish his sentence. Neil suspected that she'd followed his thought process. To his regret, her animation seemed to fade. But only briefly. Soon she was her bubbly self again. With her resilient personality, she seldom stayed quiet and pensive for long.

Would he ever tire of her company? Neil didn't think so. It would be kind if he did during this sham honeymoon. Or at least during the duration of the sham marriage.

The real danger, he knew, was developing a routine in which she was his companion away from the store. Then after Sophia had passed away and the marriage was dissolved, he would have to get used to being alone again.

Neil needed to keep reminding himself that the companionship was temporary, just like the marriage.

They'd brought along a few supplies for stocking the pantry and refrigerator in the cabin they'd rented, but at Cara's suggestion they stopped off at a supermarket when they'd neared their destination. Neil normally disliked doing grocery shopping, but he found himself having fun helping her select fresh fruit and snacks and food for meals, too.

"When are we going to eat all this?" he asked laughingly as the grocery cart started to fill up. "I figured we would go out to restaurants for most of our meals."

"Didn't I ever mention I'm a supermarketaholic?"

"So I can expect a full refrigerator while we're housemates?"

"Probably chock-a-block full. And the freezer, too. I can't help myself. When I run across two-for-one specials, I buy two of this, two of that."

"You have a lot of room to work with, starting off," he said. His refrigerator and freezer had probably never even been half-filled.

"I'll try to restrain myself."

"Not on my account." They were standing side by side at the apple bin. Neil circled her shoulders and hugged her, tender affection welling up. "If buying food makes you happy, sweetheart, buy away."

He felt pretty damn close to happy himself right at the moment. That realization might have been more sobering if Neil figured there was a real danger of his falling into the trap of believing that the feeling of "life is great" could last.

It was okay to be happy on a temporary basis.

The last few miles of the drive to the cabin took them on a two-lane mountain highway with forests on both sides. "Smell the air," Cara exclaimed. "It's all scented with trees and wildflowers and the lake. I wish we could bottle some and take it home with us!"

They had the windows rolled down, and Neil was sucking in lungfuls, too. "The air's great, all right," he said. "We might get spoiled by low humidity and cool temperatures in June."

"I hope the cabin's as nice as the pictures in the brochure, but even if it isn't, I'm not sorry we picked northern Alabama, are you? We could sleep in a tent in this kind of climate. Make that two tents side by side," she added.

Neil decided to ignore the tinge of regret in her tone over a provision for separate sleeping accommodations. He was clearing away the image of the two of them snuggled together in a sleeping bag. "The cabin's probably every bit as nice as the pictures. Plus it has a bathroom. Tents don't come equipped with bathrooms. Or running water."

"Have you ever been tent-camping?"

"Sure. When I was a kid."

"I never have. It always seemed fun, sitting around a campfire, roughing it. Oh, look, there's a trailhead. That's one of the trails we said we would hike, remember?"

Neil had noticed the small wooden sign at the edge of the woods, too. "You're right. I recognize the name."

"I bought hiking boots."

She'd gotten sidetracked, and her mind was on hiking now, much to Neil's relief. It was so hard for him to deny her anything she wanted that he had in his power to give her. He had been on the verge of saying, "We can take a weekend camping trip this fall."

By this fall Cara's grandmother might have passed away, leaving Cara free once more to get on with her life. She should find some other man to introduce her to camping, not him. A man who could share a sleeping bag with her. Neil disliked that unknown man intensely.

Just as he'd disliked Roy Xavier intensely.

I *was* jealous of Xavier, Neil admitted to himself. The flash of insight was all the more disturbing since it cast his opposition to Cara's recent romance in a whole different light. Just how fair had he been in sizing up Xavier as a potential husband for Cara?

Neil saved the introspection for later. He suspected there would be plenty of time for soul-searching during hours he should be sleeping.

They turned off the highway onto a paved access road. When the cabin came into sight, Cara described it for Neil as though he weren't taking in the details himself approvingly. "It looks exactly what a cabin on a lake should look like, doesn't it? Weatherbeaten exterior, simple architecture. Nestled under big shade trees with a wonderful backdrop of open water."

"Do you suppose the real-estate rental people hired that fisherman to drift by in his boat and complete the whole scene?" asked Neil, tongue in cheek.

She laughed and punched him lightly on the arm. "You think it's great, too."

"I confess. I think it's great." Neil could have added that a couple on a real honeymoon couldn't have asked for a more ideal hideaway, with not a neighbor in sight on either side.

When they pulled up in front of the cabin and stopped, she had her door open and was out of the car almost before Neil killed the engine.

"Let's take a walk and stretch our legs before we lug our stuff inside," she urged.

"I can lug the stuff in by myself."

"Come *on*." She grabbed his hand. Neil gave in without any resistance and accompanied her. They circled the cabin, strolling toward the lake. "Oh, look!"

Cara exclaimed. "Our own private little floating dock, just like the picture in the brochure!"

"I knew you were dying to see that dock," he said with amusement.

"How did you guess?" Her smile was a sheepish confession.

"It's the feature that sold you on this cabin instead of the other one we were considering, right?"

"You know me too well."

"I should know you well after twenty-nine years, don't you think?"

Neil was glad they'd taken the walk, glad they were having this conversation, which re-established the old comfortable status quo, before they took up residence in their honeymoon quarters. Coming up was night two of being married and sleeping in separate beds.

Despite his lack of sleep the previous night, he wasn't feeling nearly as fatigued as he would need to feel when bedtime came.

The cabin interior passed inspection just as easily as the outside appearance and location had. Neil seconded Cara's approval of the cleanliness and the snug, homey atmosphere of the main room, a combination living room, dining area and kitchen. Hooked rugs adorned the planked wooden floor, and the pine furniture with chintz cushions looked sturdy and inviting.

Next they checked out the bedrooms. As pictured in the brochure, one was furnished with a queen-size bed and the other with twin beds. Cara entered each room and stroked the patchwork quilt coverlets, declaring, ''Aren't these pretty?'' Embroidered runners on the pine dressers also drew her pleased notice.

Neil remained at the doorways. He mainly wanted to get the awkward business of room assignments over with.

''Why don't you take this bedroom?'' he suggested. She was standing inside the one with the queen-size bed.

''No, I'll take the other one. A queen-size bed is a little longer than a single bed. Besides, I can use that extra bed to toss clothes on. It'll be just like those weekends when my college roommate went home.''

Nothing at all like a honeymoon.

''Neil, that wasn't a dig at you,'' she said quickly, coming over to him, her expression contrite.

''I know it wasn't. No need to apologize. You were just being your usual sweet self and making the most of a crummy situation.''

''Not so crummy.'' She kissed him on the cheek and brushed by him, her breasts grazing his arm. ''I think I'll go ahead and unpack.''

''Let me carry your suitcases.'' He'd deposited them outside in the main room minutes earlier.

''No need to. They have wheels.''

Neil didn't heed her refusal. The least he could do was manhandle her luggage.

''How about grilled steaks for dinner?'' suggested Cara. She'd finished unpacking and had joined Neil in the living room.

"I figured we'd try the lodge restaurant at the state park."

"Oh. Okay. That'll be fun." Cara hid her disappointment. She'd had visions of the two of them sitting out on their back porch and drinking a cold beer or a glass of wine while they enjoyed the view and had a laid-back evening. But he apparently preferred going out. There would be other nights, she reminded herself as she went to change into a skirt and blouse and freshen up her makeup.

When she emerged, Neil had donned a sports jacket.

The lodge turned out to be a massive building perched on a wooded hillside. They entered the lobby, whose lofty ceilings accentuated the sense of spaciousness. The restaurant was located on a lower level. On the way to a set of broad stairs, Cara pulled Neil to a stop.

"Hello there," she said to a black bear that had been preserved by a taxidermist. The animal was lifelike enough to have ambled right out of the woods into the lodge.

"I hope we don't run into one of his kinfolk on our hikes," Neil remarked.

"If we do, we'll just hand over lunch and leave."

"Strikes me as a good plan."

Cara laughed at his rueful expression, and they descended the stairs, side by side, her arm linked in his. The restaurant was an immense dark-timbered room with the same high ceilings as the lobby and the same rustic lodge ambience. A friendly hostess led them past a large stone fireplace to a table draped in a tablecloth with cloth napkins artfully folded for a touch of elegance.

Seated comfortably across from Neil, a candle flickering in a glass holder in the center of the table, Cara breathed out a happy sigh. "This is nice, isn't it?"

He smiled at her. "Let's just hope the food's as good as the atmosphere."

"It will be."

Her optimistic prediction proved true. The only complaint wasn't really a complaint—portions of each course tended to be too liberal, starting off with a tossed green salad topped with creamy homemade dressing. Neither Cara nor Neil could consume all of the roast chicken and mashed potatoes with gravy on their dinner plates.

"I wish I had room for peach cobbler à la mode, but I don't," Cara regretfully informed the waitress after the matronly woman had listed the tempting selection of desserts for that evening.

"Let's have a cup of coffee and then reconsider our dessert option," Neil suggested to Cara.

Coffee sounded good, and she was more than willing to linger a few minutes longer.

They ended up staying more than a few minutes. After one cup of coffee, Neil ordered a dessert for them to share. They ate it slowly. When he accepted a refill on his coffee, she did the same. At some point, Cara began to suspect that he might be dawdling in order to put off returning to the cabin. Why? Because he was probably dreading their second night under the same roof. Cara was sympathetic but her good mood had fizzled on her, nonetheless.

Finally they paid the bill and left, the last party in the restaurant.

In the car she tilted her head back against the headrest.

"Tired?" Neil asked. Unless it was her imagination, he seemed hopeful.

Cara was glad she could honestly answer in the affirmative. Although her fatigue was a matter of spirit as well as body. "Yes. What about you?"

"I'm a little tired, too."

"We should make an early night of it and wake up full of energy tomorrow."

"Suits me," he said with alacrity.

The moon was nearly full and shed a luminous light on the lake when they got out of the car at the cabin. Cara wished he would suggest a walk around the back to their little private dock. The night was too beautiful not to stay outdoors at least a short while and enjoy being a part of nature.

But Neil apparently wasn't on the same wavelength. He made no such suggestion. Cara knew he would humor her if she spoke up, but she didn't want to be humored. Smothering her dissatisfaction, she accompanied him inside in the cabin.

"Would you like to watch TV?" Neil asked. "A couple of stations come in fairly clearly." He'd checked out the TV reception earlier when he'd finished his unpacking before Cara finished hers.

"No, I believe I'll take a book to bed with me and read a couple of chapters."

He didn't try to dissuade her from that solitary plan.

"Good night." Cara came close to give him a kiss on the cheek. When his arms came around her, she hugged him around the waist.

"I'm sorry," he said, his voice heavy with apology. "Going on a fake honeymoon is a drag, isn't it?"

She bit her lip because she wanted so badly to answer, It doesn't have to be a fake honeymoon. It could be a real honeymoon. But she didn't need to point that fact out to him. He knew the situation. "Why should you be sorry?" she said. "I'm the one who cooked up this whole phony marriage, remember?"

"Sooner or later you'll find a guy who'll make you a great husband. And I promise you I won't interfere like I did with Roy."

Cara pulled back to look into his face. "You're not blaming yourself for my breakup with Roy?"

"Not entirely, but I figure my bias against him was a negative factor."

"Your instincts were right on target. I didn't tell you this before, but Roy has a violent streak in him. During our final conversation, if you can call it that, he drew his fist back and scared me silly."

"Why, that—cowardly lug—" Cara could tell that Neil was mentally calling Roy far worse names, names that would have been bleeped out on radio or TV news coverage.

"He didn't hit me," she hastened to assure him. "But I realized he was capable of it. So don't feel guilty for any role you played in the breakup. You did me a favor."

"The guy had better stay out of my store. If he has the nerve to walk in there—"

"You'll give him the cool, polite treatment," Cara stated. "Promise me you won't act on what I've told you." He didn't answer, and his jaw was set so hard the muscles were ridged. "Promise me."

Finally he nodded in response to her plea.

Cara relaxed. Neil wouldn't break his word. She didn't have to worry about an ugly scene between him and Roy the next time they encountered each other.

"Now don't brood about Roy," Cara scolded Neil as she left him in the living room after another goodnight kiss on the cheek.

"I won't," he replied. "If it won't disturb you, I'll watch TV for a few minutes."

"It won't bother me at all."

Neil turned on the TV and sat back on the sofa, certain that he'd never been more wide awake in his entire life. The caffeine in the coffee he'd drunk probably hadn't helped to make him sleepy. Nor had Cara's revelation about Roy Xavier's balling up his fist at her. He seethed with anger and disgust at the no-good car salesman. In Neil's code of male behavior, a man wasn't brutish to a woman, period, and especially not to a woman he cared enough about to marry.

Learning about the incident had aroused a fierce protectiveness in him. He hated that Cara had been subjected to fear, to ugliness, to possible harm. How was he to guard against anything similar happening in the future when she was single again and dating men who might turn out to be Roy Xaviers?

Don't set her free. Keep her as your wife.

Sure. Keep Cara safe from harm like you did Lisa, Neil thought, his anger and disgust suddenly directed at himself. He'd felt strongly protective toward his first wife, his real wife. He'd felt strongly protective toward their little son. And he'd been totally helpless to guard them from danger.

These past three years he'd struggled to cope with his helplessness. His devastating loss. His bitterness. His anger. Tonight all those gut-wrenching emotions boiled up, proving he hadn't come to terms with his grief nearly as well as he'd believed he had done.

Some husband he would make Cara. She deserved a better man, a stronger man. A whole man. The least Neil could do to protect her was look out for her welfare and not let her confuse deep affection for him as romantic man-woman love.

Cara lay propped in her single bed, fighting the urge to slip on a robe and join Neil in the living room. If he had wanted her company, he would have asked her to watch TV with him. He hadn't.

Finally the low hum of the TV abruptly stopped and she heard the quiet sounds that signaled he was retiring for the night. Water running in the bathroom. The muted click of his bedroom door closing. Cara blew out a noisy breath of relief.

And letdown.

Now maybe she could concentrate on the storyline of her novel. A romance novel, her preferred reading for entertainment and no apologies, thank you very much.

The author was one of her favorites, a wonderful storyteller, and Cara was soon engrossed in the New England setting and the interaction between the hero and spunky heroine. Several chapters later, she still hadn't gotten sleepy, so she kept on reading.

The hour grew later, and, finally, at midnight, Cara put down her book, mindful that Neil was getting his rest. Tomorrow was another day, and she wanted to feel well-rested herself when she got up in the morning.

Quietly she tiptoed to the bathroom. No sounds of snoring came from Neil's bedroom. Did he snore? she wondered. The flushing of the toilet sounded incredibly loud in the quiet cabin. Cara cringed at the noise. Back in her bedroom, she turned off the lamp and got into bed.

And lay there, wide awake. Reading hadn't lulled her mind. Or her body, for that matter. She'd enjoyed the sensual scenes between the male and female characters too much. If Neil were to come into her bedroom, ready to become her bridegroom in reality, he would definitely find her responsive, Cara reflected with longing.

Hugging herself, she fantasized. *Her bedroom door opened. Neil spoke her name in a low voice that made goose bumps of pleasure pop out on her skin. "Cara?" She answered him breathlessly, "Yes, Neil."*

It was enough communication. Enough invitation. He walked swiftly over to the bed, got under the covers with her, drew her close in a strong, passionate embrace. She could feel his aroused body, sense how urgently he wanted her....

Cara groaned aloud and sat up. Did the cold shower remedy work for women? She didn't dare try it out, for fear of waking Neil up. Maybe an ice-cold soft drink would cool her off.

Her eyes were used to the darkness, which was only semi-darkness since the chintz curtains at the windows didn't totally block out the bright moonlight. Cara could see well enough not to bother snapping on the lamp. She tiptoed, barefoot, from her bedroom and made her way without mishap to the refrigerator.

After surveying her choices, she selected a citrus-flavored soft drink without caffeine. Conscious of not wanting to make any noise, she grasped the pop-top ring and tugged ever so gently, but the sound of carbonation escaping from the can was still a mini explosion. Cara tensed, grimacing. When long seconds ticked by, and Neil didn't emerge from his bedroom, she took a sip of her soft drink—and swallowed wrong so that she had to cough!

Again Cara froze, like a statue, her hand clapped over her mouth. More seconds ticked by. Thank heaven she must not have disturbed Neil because all was quiet in the cabin.

Through the windows in the dining area Cara could see onto the screened back porch. It was softly illuminated by silvery moonlight. She could even make out the stripes of the chair cushions.

Surely it would be safe enough to go out there and finish her soft drink, Cara reasoned. She wasn't ready yet to return to her bedroom, and this wide-open main room was like an echo chamber.

On her trip to the door leading onto the porch, Cara was certain her bare feet managed to find every creaky plank in the floor. Unlocking the door involved a lot of clicks that made her wince. Then the hinges squeaked. Eventually she was out on the porch, and all the agony of getting there proved worthwhile.

The cool air soothed her case of nerves, and the view of the lake silvered by moonlight entranced Cara. Somewhere out in the water a large fish splashed. Cara breathed in and breathed out, tension ebbing from her body. The chorus of night critters seemed a friendly cacophony.

"You can't sleep either?" Neil asked.

Cara was lifting her soft drink to her lips, so in tune

with nature that she hadn't heard him come to the open door behind her. When he spoke, she shrieked in surprise and dropped her can. It struck the floor and rolled away from her, following the downward slant of the porch and pouring out liquid.

"Sorry. I didn't mean to scare you." Neil came over toward her as he apologized. Cara saw that he was wearing the bottoms of the knit pajamas. From the waist up he wore nothing. The sight of his naked upper torso didn't help to slow her hammering pulse.

"I guess I woke you, making all that noise," she said.

"You didn't wake me. I hadn't fallen asleep." He picked up the can and then set it upright on the floor and left it there. "Want me to get you another soft drink? That one's empty."

"No, thanks. I'd had enough." Thirst was low on Cara's list of wants and needs. The moonlight seemed to have brightened, making her self-consciously aware that she hadn't slipped a robe over her silk nightgown. "The lake is so beautiful all bathed in moonlight, isn't it?" she said. Her voice came out breathy and excited.

"Beautiful." He was gazing at her. "Aren't you cold?" Before Cara could reply, he reached out and touched her shoulder as though determining the answer for himself. Momentarily her heart stopped beating as he kept his hand there. His palm was warm against her skin.

"A little," she answered. "What about you?" Following his example, she lifted her fingertips to his chest. He sucked in his breath audibly.

"Are you kidding? Cold with you dressed in that thin nightgown, looking even sexier than I'd imagined." He cupped her other shoulder and both hands moved with a caressing motion.

Cara went weak in the knees, weathering delicate ripples of pleasure. She could feel her nipples hardening and poking against silk. "I thought you were sound asleep," she said. "Otherwise I would have given some thought to modesty." She brought her other hand to his chest and stroked the taut, manly contours. "Speaking of sexy, you're quite a hunk in those topless pj's."

"I didn't take the time to put the top on. When I heard you unlocking the door, I didn't want you going outside by yourself." While he made the explanation, he was sliding his hands up and down her back, creating heat that threatened to burn away Cara's conscience. Why not let him continue and allow things to take their course? She hadn't deliberately lured him out here on the moonlit porch to seduce him.

No, but you promised to play fair, and you should.

"Neil, you're turning me on," Cara confided softly. "Not that I'm complaining. You should know, though, that I came out here to cool off."

"To cool off?"

"My novel I was reading had some steamy sex scenes. Then when I turned off the light, I started thinking about you and got all hot and bothered."

"Thanks for telling me that." His tone was pained and ironic. He took her hands and placed them at his waist, then gathered her into his arms and hugged her, evidently his way of calling a halt to risky foreplay. Cara hugged him back. The embrace was hardly a cure for her escalating excitement, though, not with her breasts pressing against his chest and her nipples more stimulated than before by the contact.

Though farther down her lower body wasn't welded to his—Neil was making an effort to avoid the most intimate proximity—she could definitely feel for herself now what had been evident to the eye in the moonlight. Neil was physically ready to make love to her, if only he *wanted* to in his heart and mind.

Obviously he didn't, and that knowledge hurt, despite understanding the reasons. Her sense of rejection helped more than anything else to douse passion.

"I can satisfy you, Cara. There are ways other than making love. Let me—"

"No. I'll be okay. Honest. Don't worry about me." She pressed a kiss to his jaw. Her movement made her breasts rub against the hard wall of his chest. Delicious sensations shot through her, sensations that almost overwhelmed resolutions about not seducing him against his will.

Neil groaned and tightened his arms, immobilizing her. "You're so luscious. So sexy. Keeping my hands off you is probably the biggest test of character of my whole life. But it wouldn't be right, Cara. It wouldn't be good for you. For either of us."

"By good, you mean beneficial."

"Of course, that's what I mean. *Good* wouldn't even begin to describe the sexual pleasure I would get."

"But afterwards you wouldn't be glad. I couldn't stand that." She sighed.

"It kills me to see you unhappy over anything. It always has." He rubbed his cheek against her head and kissed her hair. They stood there, holding each other, at an impasse. What else was there to say or do? Cara struggled to control the urge to cry and won.

"We can't waste this moonlight," she said. "Since sex is out, why don't we put on our robes and take a walk?"

"Where? Down to your little dock?" His tone was teasing and full of loving indulgence. It was clear he *did* care for her. Things *might* work out eventually. They *had* to.

"You get an *A*."

Camaraderie was restored, allowing them to pretend once again that the sexual chemistry didn't exist.

"Good. You did pack a cotton robe," Neil said when Cara stepped out onto the porch a few minutes later, belted into a pink-and-white-striped seersucker robe. He sounded greatly relieved. Evidently he'd had fears of her appearing in a negligee.

She held her arms wide and did a pirouette. "Doesn't it look like something Alice Cramden would wear on that old TV classic, 'The Honeymooners'? It's my 'throw on in case of a fire in the middle of the night' robe.'' With her new supply of beautiful peignoirs, she'd had to force herself to pack the darn homely thing.

"Alice wouldn't look that cute.''

"Thanks. I guess.''

He'd donned his pajama top as well as his robe. Like her, he'd put on shoes instead of slippers.

Once they'd left the porch via the screen door Neil unlatched and held open, Cara slipped her arm in his. They strolled across the moonlit lawn to the dock and walked out on it. The surface of the huge lake was like molten silver.

"Just think. We could be sleeping now,'' Cara mused. "We would miss this.''

"It's a great night, all right.''

The time seemed right to delve into his resistance to deepening their relationship. "Could we have a serious conversation?'' she asked.

"About what?''

"About us.''

"Sure.'' His agreement lacked enthusiasm, but at least he'd given her the go-ahead.

"Are you still shocked at the idea that you're sexually attracted to me? You know, after regarding me as sort of a little adopted sister for so many years?''

"The shock has worn off,'' he admitted.

"So you don't feel a sense of impropriety now?''

"I feel less a sense of impropriety as time goes on.''

So far, so good, Cara thought. She moved along.

"So if you woke up tomorrow and decided you'd changed your mind about not remarrying—"

"That's not going to happen," he put in before she could finish her sentence.

"We're just dealing with hypotheticals. My point is you wouldn't rule me out as a prospective wife because of our history?"

"You would be at the top of the list. Okay?"

"I would?" Cara had to pause a moment and absorb the thrill of her eligibility.

"Shall we call it a night now?" Neil asked. "It's one-thirty."

"Could I touch on one more issue first? Please." She hadn't meant to lose the momentum of the important discussion.

He conceded with his silence.

"As I understand it, your reason for not remarrying and having another family is that you couldn't bear losing another wife and child. But in my case, you already love me, and I'm a part of your life. Whether or not we were married, you would grieve if I died. Right?"

"Cara, it's knowing how much I would grieve *now* that kept me out of your bedroom tonight. Can't you understand that? Of course, you can't," he answered his own question.

"Help me understand! You would love me more if I were your real wife? That's what you saying?"

"Not just more. Differently. Love between a married couple is special. It really is a holy bond. There're no holds barred. There's no protection whatever against losing this person you're totally committed to in a blink of an eye. I'm sorry, but I won't—I can't—make myself that kind of sitting duck again." He shook his head hard.

"But you wouldn't trade those happy years with Lisa, would you? You wouldn't trade being a dad? Aren't the memories worth a lot?"

"The memories tear me apart. I block them out any way I can. There are TV shows I've never watched again, foods I've stopped eating. Why do you think I was against a honeymoon in Gulf Shores with a condo on the beach?" That had been Cara's first proposal. "Because Lisa and I headed for the ocean on vacations. So you see why we have to stick to our original bargain, Cara? I can't make you the kind of husband you want. The kind of husband you deserve."

The moonlit lake was every bit as beautiful, but the enchantment and delight were gone, leached out by discouragement. Cara wished now she'd tabled the discussion until a later time.

"I won't rock the boat, Neil. I promise. Shall we go inside?"

"Are you okay?" he asked gently.

"I'm winding down. This long day is catching up with me."

"Sleep in tomorrow morning."

"I may do that."

His solicitousness only deepened Cara's despair and sense of rejection. Neil didn't love her with the same depth and passion that he'd loved Lisa or he would find the courage to be a husband again. He loved Cara, but wasn't *in love* with her. Like she was *in love* with him.

That was the real truth at the heart of his resistance. What could Cara do?

Chapter Ten

"Hmm. What a delicious aroma." A yawn cut off Cara's last word.

Neil was standing at the stove with his back to her. He wanted like the devil to look around, but he continued turning slices of bacon in a skillet. In her sleepy state, she might have wandered out of her bedroom in her nightgown, and it wouldn't do to start the day off by getting all hot and aroused. Her drowsy voice was stimulation enough. "Can I interest you in some bacon and eggs for breakfast?" he asked.

"Can you ever. Do I have time for a quick shower?"

"Sure. Don't rush. I'm just about to slide the pan of biscuits into the oven. According to the baking instructions, they'll take between twelve and fifteen minutes.''

"Biscuits, too? This is a four-star breakfast you're cooking up here. I could get spoiled awfully fast if you serve me breakfast in the mornings when we get back to Louisiana,'' she warned.

"My usual fare on a working day is dry cereal and milk."

"Yuk. Don't pour any dry cereal in my bowl. I'll stick with my yogurt and fruit. Or peanut butter on toast.''

"Double yuk," Neil said. Her giggle in response to his disgust brought a smile to his lips.

"I'll be back in plenty of time to set the table," she promised.

He couldn't help himself. He turned around and treated himself to watching her make a beeline for the bathroom, small bare feet padding on the wooden floor. She was wearing the modest robe she'd appeared in last night. In the daylight he could see the material was a pale-pink-and-white stripe. Belted tightly around her small waist, the robe didn't manage to hide her rounded bottom. Neil focused instead on her dishevelled mop of glossy black curls.

When the bathroom door closed behind her, he turned back to the stove, exercising all his willpower to shut down his male imagination and concentrate on his cooking. Neil didn't need the torture of letting himself visualize Cara stripping naked and stepping under the warm spray of the shower.

Whereas earlier he'd been careful not to make a lot of noise, he did just the opposite now, banging and clattering. He even whistled a tune for the sake of distraction.

No, not just for the sake of distraction. Neil was whistling a tune—and he'd stopped whistling the last three years—because he felt so damn good. He felt happy, as he had yesterday in the supermarket.

And why not feel a little happy and relaxed? Neil reasoned. He was on vacation with Cara, the person whose company he enjoyed more than anyone else's. Last night he'd gotten through night two of the honeymoon with nothing happening. Or nothing *much* happening. Everything was under control.

This wasn't happy-ever-after kind of happy. Just your occasional, lighthearted happy.

"I'm back," Cara said after she'd been gone about ten minutes. The announcement wasn't necessary. Neil was inhaling her clean, flowery fragrance.

"Good. The biscuits are almost done."

"They smell heavenly." She came up beside him, and Neil smiled at her, taking in her fresh-scrubbed appearance. Self-consciously she touched a lock of her damp curls. "I didn't take the time to do my hair or put on makeup."

"You look cute and every bit of sixteen." *Adorable* would have been a better description. Neil bent down to give her a kiss on the cheek. Instead he found himself veering to her soft, unpainted mouth. Just a quick peck on the lips to say good morning. No lust allowed. That's what he had in mind.

And that's the way the kiss played out. He didn't get hard or aroused. He didn't want to pick her up and carry to the nearest bedroom. Instead he was flooded by an almost unbearable sweetness as his lips met hers. From Cara's expression, he could tell she'd probably been affected the same way.

Neil wanted to kiss her again just as gently, wanted to touch her. Cherish her. With tenderness. With love.

Romantic love. Cupids and arrows and sentimental valentines. Goofy happiness. A bigger danger than lust any day in the week. Neil was furious at himself for being waylaid like this, resentful that he didn't dare even express his affection without being on guard.

"The plates are in this cabinet," he said, jerking open the upper cabinet door. He handed her two plates.

She took them and stood there a moment while he emptied a bowl of beaten eggs into a skillet, scraping the bowl as though it had done something to offend him.

Neil was braced for her to ask what was wrong with him, but she carried the plates over to the table without comment on his behavior. Quite possibly she'd put two and two together and figured out his problem for herself. She could read him better than anyone else, even his parents.

It would come so naturally to love her with one hundred percent of his heart and soul. And maybe Neil could even find the courage, except for knowing that Cara deserved a husband whose heart and soul hadn't been through the mill, as his had. Plus she wanted a family badly. That left Neil out of the picture. He definitely couldn't handle fatherhood. Not again.

If there were any doubt in his mind, all he had to do was remember a small hand nestled trustingly in his big hand and a childish voice calling him "Daddy."

"Am I dressed okay to go hiking in the woods?" Cara asked, glancing down at herself with an uncertain air. She wore red cotton slacks and a white blouse. On her feet were lace-up shoes that had to be the most feminine version of hiking boots Neil had ever seen. "I thought jeans would be hot for June," she explained, eyeing his jeans and short-sleeved knit shirt. "Probably khaki pants would have been more outdoorsy, but khaki seemed so drab for summer."

"The way you're dressed is fine. With luck, we won't see another soul."

"I wasn't worried about other people."

Comprehension dawned, making him more indulgent and amused. "Are you thinking about meeting up with Mr. Bear's relatives?"

She looked sheepish, but still slightly anxious. "For all we know, bears might react to red like bulls are supposed to do. Maybe that's why khaki got so popular for hiking clothes."

"I've never read anything about bears—or other

wild animals—reacting to bright colors. If that were a real danger, I'm sure there would be cautions for hikers to wear drab clothing.''

''You're right.''

Neil couldn't resist teasing her. ''I just hope these local bears haven't been fed a lot of juicy red apples,'' he said, deadpan.

Cara balled up a small fist and socked him on the arm as punishment, but she couldn't maintain a pretense of indignation. Her sense of humor got the best of her and she smiled in response to his broad grin.

The small incident relieved the tension that had spoiled their late breakfast. They drove to the trailhead and set out on the two-mile hike they'd selected for the day's outing. Neil carried a small backpack with bottles of water, a camera and a package of trail mix for snacking. Cara carried a trail map.

''I didn't realize we'd have to walk single file like this,'' she said after they'd been tramping along for about five minutes with Neil following behind her, enjoying her chatter.

''The view from back here is nice,'' he replied. ''I need to get the camera out and take a picture.''

''Of what?'' She stopped and gazed to the right and then to the left. ''You mean an artsy shot of those little purple wildflowers?''

Neil had caught up with her. ''No, a picture of you in those red pants.'' He patted her firm, rounded bottom. Big mistake, he knew instantly and had to pull his hand away before he could follow up the pats with a caress.

Cara's eyes had opened wide with her surprise that he'd touched a part of her body he never touched, even playfully. "Don't you dare take a picture of my backside!" she exclaimed. Her cheeks were flushed a lovely shade of pink, and she couldn't have looked prettier, sweeter, or more desirable if she'd tried.

Neil wanted to kiss her so damn bad. Both kinds of kisses. The tender kind and the hungry kind. He wanted to hug her. Both kinds of hugs, gentle and passionate. This was just great. Now he was being hit by a double whammy, lust and Cupid. It was hard enough fighting them off separately.

"Thirsty?" he asked, desperate for some diversion. He pulled out a bottle of water and offered it to her. She took a sip and gave the bottle back to him. He tilted it and drank several gulps.

"You walk in front," Cara directed.

"Okay, but don't lag too far back. And tell me to slow down if I walk too fast."

The new arrangement worked better for Neil. Or at least it worked better until she said, "Hold up a minute, will you? I'd like to get the camera out."

He stopped and looked around. The terrain hadn't changed. There wasn't much to photograph except tree trunks and underbrush and wild flowers here and there.

Cara's mock innocent expression gave him his clue a split second before she patted him on the rear. "Why haven't I ever noticed before what nice buns you have?'' she said and slipped her hand in his rear pocket.

"Smart aleck." Reckless impulse took hold of Neil and stripped away caution and wisdom. He meted out punishment with a brief, hard kiss on her mouth. Immediate concern that he'd been too rough and might have bruised her soft lips drew his head down again for a gentle, tender kiss. Flooded by the same sweet sensation he'd experienced earlier in the day, he couldn't seem to stop himself from gathering her close in his arms. Her arms went up around his neck, the trail map fluttering to the ground.

"I love the way you kiss me," she murmured, sounding like she was on cloud nine. Her voice was a huge turn-on even while it tapped into his well of tenderness. Lust and Cupid had joined into a partnership.

Stop, all Neil's instincts of self-preservation were telling him, but he didn't listen. Other instincts were stronger. After all they were in the middle of the woods. What could happen?

"Which way? Like this?" He kissed her hard. "Or this?" He nuzzled his mouth against hers, savoring the sweet intimacy.

"Both ways." She drew his head down.

This was a whole new ball game with Cara kissing him, lovingly and then passionately. Then they were kissing each other, and Neil was aware of control slipping away. But it was impossible to be sorry, as the pleasure grew more intense and then hot and sexual as their tongues mated.

Cara uttered little needy moans in her throat that incited Neil's own need and also incited that ever-present urge to make her happy. Her fingers dug into his shoulders as though making their own plea. His muscles bunched in response and the reflex seemed to free his hands. Neil slid his palms down her back and caressed her buttocks. Roughly. Gently. That devastating combination of carnal lust and protective love.

She arched closer, pressing her hips against his lower body. Neil picked her up and held her against him, sharing his hard arousal, telling her by his actions, I want you so damn much.

His breathing had become labored and the blood pounded in his ears. Otherwise he might have heard the voices and footsteps of other hikers sooner. Cara must have been similarly hearing-impaired because Neil could tell she picked up the conversation between a man and a woman at the same time he did.

"—go by the club and make a tee time for tomorrow?"

"That's a good idea."

"I'm looking forward to playing this golf course at the state park."

"Me, too."

Cara and Neil had stopped kissing. He lowered her to the ground, and they both looked in the direction they'd been heading. A fiftyish couple were in clear sight on the trail and had obviously spotted them.

"Hello there," the woman greeted them in a mid-western accent. Her blue eyes twinkled with amusement.

"Hello." Neil's answering greeting came in unison with Cara's. They edged off the trail to make room for the two to pass.

"Nice day," the man said.

"Isn't it though?" Cara replied. Neil didn't need to look at her to know she was blushing.

"Great weather," he said.

"Enjoy your hike," the woman bade them.

"Thanks." Another answer in unison.

Cara clapped a hand over her mouth to smother her giggle as the pair tramped on, single file. The comic element didn't escape Neil, but the self-disgust he was feeling stifled any urge to laugh. The way he'd carried on with Cara was no laughing matter.

He picked up the fallen trail map and handed it to her. "Ready to continue our hike?"

She gazed into his face questioningly. What she read made dismay replace the mirth that had bubbled up. "You're not already on a guilt trip, I hope."

"Don't you think I should be? I don't know what got into me, Cara. I set up rules and then I break them."

"Maybe the rules are the problem," she said and set off on the trail, walking ahead of him. Although *trudging* was a better description of her gait, and the slope of her shoulders bespoke despondency. It was all too easy to imagine big tears welling in her brown eyes and rolling down her cheeks. The image was unbearable for Neil.

"You're not crying, are you?" he asked.

"No. I'm okay." The assurance came out muffled.

"You aren't okay."

"All right. I'm not okay. It takes a while to adjust to being up in the clouds one minute and back to earth the next."

"I wish we could stay up in the clouds, Cara."

"You were up there, too?"

"Do you have to ask?"

She soon perked up. Neil wanted to stop her on the path and hug her for being such a trooper. But he'd crossed over boundaries today and might have destroyed the old brother-sister relationship forever. It was a sad and troubling possibility because he still needed those warm, innocent hugs and pats and kisses on the cheek as much as ever.

Or maybe more than ever before.

"Judging from the parking lot, the Catfish House is sure popular," said Neil. He nosed into a narrow space between a sports utility vehicle and a pickup.

"I hope the food's as good as Catfish Charlie's in Hammond. I'm starving. Again."

"You got a lot of exercise today."

"For some reason it didn't dawn on me that a two-mile hike would end up being four miles, round trip. Not until we turned around and started back."

"You did great."

"I wouldn't have missed that wonderful little babbling brook and those whole thickets of wildflowers. I hope our pictures come out."

They'd gotten out of the car and were strolling toward the restaurant, hand in hand. Cara sighed happily. There was no guessing what her state of mind would be thirty minutes from now, but at this moment she was back in the optimistic mode. She just *knew* things would work out for her and Neil.

Inside the restaurant fifteen or twenty people were waiting to be seated, but it turned out they comprised two large parties. "I have a table for two," the hostess said and beckoned Cara and Neil to follow her. Their route took them through one large dining room into another room just as large. Several long tables were occupied by what appeared to be entire families of several generations. *Family* was definitely the key word for the patrons of the Catfish House. The number of children almost equalled that of the adults.

"Quite a contrast to the lodge restaurant," Neil commented when they were facing each across a checkered oilcloth tablecloth, laminated menus in front of them. He picked up a paper-napkin-wrapped bundle of eating utensils to emphasis his point.

"This has a homey atmosphere all its own," Cara replied. She smiled at a cute little towheaded boy at a nearby table who was waving at her and trying to get her attention. Both his parents were busy, tending to twin siblings in high chairs.

Apparently reading her friendliness as an invitation,

the child wasted no time sliding down from his chair and walking over. "Hi. My name is Jason," he said.

"Hi, Jason." She glanced at Neil and saw that he wasn't smiling. From his expression his thoughts were elsewhere, in a different place and time. A time and place that held painful memories.

"I'm three years old," Jason informed her, holding up a small hand with the correct number of fingers aloft.

"Jason, come and finish eating your supper, son." His father had noticed his absence and addressed him in a stern tone.

"I'm talking to this lady, Daddy."

"Jason."

"Okay, Daddy." But he got in as much conversation as possible as he took small steps backward. "My sisters are twins. They was borned at the same time in a hospital. I can tell them apart. That's Mindy my mommy is feeding. My daddy is feeding Mandy." Jason bumped into his chair.

His father lifted him by his waist and set him in the seat. He looked around at Cara and Neil. "I think I'm raising either a salesman or a politician," he said, shaking his head. His tone held more indulgent pride than complaint.

"We didn't mind. It was a pleasure meeting Jason," Cara assured him, aware that she couldn't really speak for Neil. He'd managed a strained smile for the father's sake, but she doubted he'd gotten any pleasure from the little boy's visit to their table. It wasn't difficult to guess why. His son had been three when he'd died in the accident.

The waitress came with their glasses of iced tea and stayed to take their food order. Cara had only glanced at the menu, but she found it easy to make a choice anyway. "I'll have the fried catfish dinner."

"Sounds good to me, too," Neil said. From his tone, he couldn't have cared less what the woman brought and set down in front of him.

"French fries or potato salad?" the waitress asked.

Cara wasn't a potato salad fan. "French fries."

"You, sir?"

"Either one."

At the risk of acting like a real wife, Cara intervened. "Wouldn't you prefer potato salad?"

"Sure. Make mine potato salad."

When the waitress was gone, he met Cara's gaze. He'd already issued a silent apology before he said, "Sorry. This happens every now and then. Something throws a switch."

She reached over and laid her hand on his. "Jason reminds you of Chris?"

He nodded. "Does he ever. When Lisa and I would take him to restaurants, he would be out of his chair like a shot and making friends with total strangers. I've said those exact same words, 'I'm raising a salesman or a politician.'" Then tragedy had struck and cut his little son's life short.

Cara's heart ached for him. She blinked hard to remove a glaze of tears and struggled to compose herself. Breaking down and crying wouldn't do any good, and yet her sadness seemed overwhelming. Suddenly Neil's hand was clasping hers in a strong, gentle grip, and she was on the receiving end, being comforted by him instead of vice versa. "Here, have a sip of your iced tea," he instructed her.

She obeyed.

"Mamma and Nonna both said to tell you hello," said Cara, laying her cell phone on the coffee table. She'd phoned home, sitting curled up at one end of the sofa while Neil sat at the other end, watching TV with the volume lowered.

"How is Sophia?"

"She sounded great. It's a good sign that she was still up this late in the evening. Nonna was always a night owl until she became so ill."

"Morale counts for so much in fighting disease. You may have prolonged your grandmother's life here on earth by granting her greatest wish—to attend your wedding."

Cara nodded, her expression serene. "Whether it was good for you or for me to put us through all this, a fake honeymoon, a fake marriage, I'm not sorry, Neil."

"That's good to know. For my part, I'd do it all over again, too."

"You would?"

"Honest."

She expelled a breath of contentment and uncurled

her legs, stretching them out on the sofa cushion and modestly re-arranging her skirt so that it didn't ride up higher than her knees. "I probably should have broken in those new hiking boots before I walked four miles in them," she said, flexing her bare feet.

Neil turned sideways and began to massage her feet. She groaned with pleasure and promptly slid lower into a reclining position, bringing her feet closer to him so that he didn't have to lean over to reach them.

"That feels wonderful," she declared, her tone blissful. She closed her eyes.

He was enjoying his ministrations as much as she was. It was deeply, quietly pleasurable to knead and stroke and caress her body in a non-erogenous zone. After he'd thoroughly massaged her arches and toes, Neil advanced to her ankles. Then to her calves.

"You may have to scrape me up with a spatula," she murmured and yawned. Within seconds she'd fallen asleep, a smile on her pretty face. Neil sat a long time and watched her, feeling more relaxed and at peace than he had in weeks.

Finally, when she didn't stir or awaken on her own, he spoke to her. "Cara, it's time to go to bed, sweetheart."

No response. He made several other attempts, even shaking her by the shoulder gently. She remained deeply asleep. Poor darling, she was probably as beat as he was, Neil reflected. Should he pick her up and carry her to bed? Or leave her there on the sofa and not disturb her? She seemed completely comfortable with her head nestled in a throw pillow.

He decided on the latter plan, but before he retired to his bedroom, he unfastened the waistband of her skirt and covered her with a soft flannel sheet he found in a linen closet.

Neil was hardly able to keep his eyes open as he stripped off his clothes and got into bed. *Maybe I'll get a decent night's sleep....*

He hardly completed the thought before he was out like a light.

Cara was confused for several seconds when she woke up at dawn. Where was she? On the sofa in the cabin. She closed her eyes again and wiggled her feet, remembering last night's massage. Neil's strong, gentle hands on her feet, her ankles, her calves. She relived the delicious sensations. Only now those sensations didn't lull her to sleep. They awoke neediness in those neglected portions of her body that hadn't been caressed and kneaded and stroked.

She moaned softly and cupped her breasts. Will he ever touch me here? she wondered. If he didn't at some point, Cara might just die of the frustration.

Flipping back the sheet, she swung her legs down and stood up. To her surprise, her skirt dropped down around her ankles. Neil must have unfastened it, Cara deduced. She stepped free, picked up the skirt and draped it over her arm. Unbuttoning her blouse, she started for her bedroom. It wasn't full daylight yet. She could lie down in bed and sleep a few more hours.

Except she wasn't sleepy.

Cara paused, slipping off her blouse. She glanced toward the kitchen, thinking, *A glass of juice would taste good.* A chair sat conveniently close. Cara deposited her outfit on it. Attired in her bra and panties, she had taken several steps toward the kitchen when a clicking sound brought her to a halt. She whirled around in time to see Neil's bedroom door opening and Neil emerging.

He wore nothing but his boxer shorts. Cara gazed with female appreciation, her pulses racing. He hadn't seen her, she realized. Rubbing his hand over his face, he veered in the direction of the bathroom. Then he dropped his hand and looked out toward the living room. Perhaps remembering that he'd left her asleep on the couch? Abruptly he stopped, midstep, catching sight of her.

"Cara." The one word expressed a multitude of emotions: surprise, love, awed male admiration. His voice held messages ranging from I adore you to I want you more than anything. She might have been an apparition out of his dreams from the way he gazed at her.

Cara opened her lips to say something in reply, but her vocal cords didn't seem to be operating normally. Not a single word came out. Perhaps she was too filled with longings that defied expression. Perhaps she was too afraid of damaging the sense of being poised on a threshold. In lieu of speaking, she took a step toward him. For one terrible second, he didn't move. Then he took a step toward her. Joy blossomed inside Cara as though her heart were staging its own Fourth of July fireworks display.

When they were close enough that he might have taken her into his arms, Neil broke the pulsing silence. "Do you know how beautiful you are?" he asked, his voice low and passionate.

Once again speech failed the usually talkative Cara. Her multiple choice answers were yes or no, and neither one was adequate as an answer. She knew she'd never felt this beautiful before in her life, never felt this desirable in any other man's eyes. She knew she might die on the spot if he didn't touch her.

Incredibly she must have communicated all that without words because Neil raised his hands and placed them on her shoulders. Cara's whole body went weak with the shock waves of delight as he caressed her skin with an exquisite gentleness. When strength returned she reached up and located his hands and brought them down to her chest. Slowly she took her hands away, issuing a mute plea, Please...

He caressed the upper curves of her breasts with his fingertips. Cara sucked in her breath and arched her back, feeling her nipples tingle as they contracted and formed hard peaks, doing their part to encourage him to continue the intimate exploration she wanted so much. Needed so much.

"You're so lush and firm." He delved a forefinger

into her cleavage, then gathered her fullness into his palms.

Cara finally found her voice when he used his thumbs to stroke her rock-like nipples. She whispered his name in bliss.

He bent and kissed the tops of her breasts. His hot breath awoke a wilder pleasure in Cara. She reached back and unhooked her bra. The straps slid down her arm and the cups loosened. Not taking any chances that Neil might straighten up, Cara clasped his head and guided him on a wonderful, maddening journey over newly bared curves. Caught somewhere between languor and urgency, she thought she might melt into a puddle of pleasure. Finally he took one nipple into his mouth, laved with his tongue, grazed with his teeth.

Languor lost out to urgency at that point. Cara's lower body had been ignored long enough. She stopped combing her fingers through Neil's hair and found his hands, which so far hadn't ventured below her waist. She carried them down to her hips, murmuring, "Please. Please."

He moved them around to her bottom, his palms sliding smoothly on the silk of her bikini panties. "I love your cute fanny," he said.

"I like your rear view a lot, too," Cara confided. She was stroking his shoulders and back, enjoying the feel of his taut muscles. She'd wanted to touch him like this since she was fifteen and he was twenty. Realizing that fantasy now compounded her adult pleasure.

Cara suffered a moment's confusion as Neil crouched down in front of her. Then her excitement escalated to a new pitch when he began kissing a path down her stomach to her abdomen. Meanwhile, he'd hooked his fingers under the elastic of her panties and was tugging them down. Cara would have helped, but she was immobilized by erotic sensations.

Neil had reached her pelvic area. Now his kisses were incredibly intimate. His lips nuzzled delicate folds and his tongue found her nub. Cara cried out helplessly, her knees buckling and parting her thighs to him. He held her by her hips, supporting her as he pleasured her, setting off spasms that rocketed through her body and made her cry out again and again

Limp as a rag doll, Cara sank down on the floor with him. Neil took her on his lap and hugged her tightly. Cara's fogged mind slowly cleared. It dawned on her what had happened. Neil had made good the offer she'd refused to satisfy her sexually without actually making love.

"That was all for me, wasn't it?" she said.

"Are you kidding? You think I didn't enjoy myself?" he chided her.

"At least let me do the same for you."

"I'm okay, sweetheart."

She could feel how "okay" he was, but Cara didn't persist. The next time she wouldn't be so selfish, though, she resolved. In a similar situation, she would follow his example and pleasure him without getting his go-ahead. Then she would see how "okay" he was.

Chapter Eleven

"I might buy this T-shirt for myself." Cara held the shirt in front of her. She and Neil were shopping for souvenirs in the gift shop of the space center in Huntsville, having driven there from Guntersville that morning to spend a fascinating and educational day.

"Isn't it too large for you?" he asked.

"I was thinking more along the lines of wearing it to sleep in," she admitted.

"Why would you sleep in a T-shirt when—" He broke off.

Cara filled in the rest of his question: "When I have a whole drawerful of pretty nightgowns? For modesty. I wouldn't have to be so careful about putting on a robe." She hesitated before giving her other reason, which was rather embarrassing to explain. "And for comfort."

"Comfort?" Since when wasn't a silk nightgown comfortable? he was probably wondering, judging from his puzzled expression.

She made a comical face. "The last thing I need is to feel sexy when I'm trying to fall asleep. And I figure it will help you to imagine me wearing something like this." She held up the T-shirt again.

"You're having trouble falling asleep?"

"Yes. Aren't you? I'll bet the only decent night's sleep either of us has gotten was our second night at the cabin when I konked out on the sofa." Remembering that dawn interlude the following morning hadn't done anything to cure insomnia as she had lain in her bed each evening since then.

Neil sighed and the fatigue showed on his face. "The strangeness will wear off when we get back home to Louisiana. We'll settle into a comfortable routine. I hope," he added.

"I'm sure we will." Cara raised on tiptoes and kissed him on the cheek. He tensed. "Neil!" she said in protest, her face still close to his. "You freeze up every time I come close to you. I can't stand it! We're used to being affectionate toward each other."

He met her reproachful gaze, apology in his eyes. "I'll work on not freezing up." He kissed her on the mouth, a tender, loving kiss that melted Cara's irritation. But also awoke the familiar longing that seemed to grow more intense with every day that passed.

"That's better," she said, smiling at him.

"Here's the problem," he said, not smiling back. His gaze dropped to her mouth. Cara's heartbeat quickened with her surge of anticipation. She closed her eyes as he lowered his head and kissed her again. Their mouths clung together.

A child's giggle penetrated her consciousness and then a woman's voice, "Come here, Sarah. Let's pick out a baseball shirt for Jimmy."

"Look, Mommy, they're *kissing*. Like you and Daddy."

Cara and Neil pulled apart reluctantly and moved away to a more private spot, near a display of mugs. "You get my point?" he asked. "We're not like sister and brother any more." His voice resonated regret.

"So where does that leave us?" she asked.

"I'm hoping that with time, we'll relax around one another again."

"You're hoping the sexual attraction will wear off?"

"Yes." He didn't sound terribly confident.

"And in the meanwhile? Am I supposed to keep my distance? Not touch you? Not hug you?"

"No, you don't have to keep your distance. But try to understand my behavior if I'm not as responsive as you'd like. One thing hasn't changed. And won't change," he stated. "I care about you as much as before."

"Same here." Cara reached up and caressed his cheek. He flinched in a reflex movement. She dropped her hand. Despite the frank discussion they'd just had, she still felt sharp rejection. "We'd better get our shopping done," she said. "It's going to cost me a fortune by the time I buy souvenirs for all my nieces and nephews."

"I'll buy the souvenirs," Neil said.

"Do you know how many nieces and nephews we're talking about?"

"Twenty-five, isn't it? I think I remember all the names." He recited them, much to Cara's amazement and added some identifying characteristic for each girl and boy.

"What a memory!" she exclaimed.

Neil shrugged. "I've been to several family get-togethers during the last couple of months since we got engaged."

He'd seemed to enjoy himself, too, and had fit in so well, Cara recalled. His interaction with her family had seemed a big plus factor. Maybe he *would* eventually want to stay married to her, given some more time. They'd been husband and wife barely a week. It was much too soon to give up. Cara's spirits lifted with one of her surges of optimism.

Together they selected T-shirts, baseball caps, model space ships, coloring books and costume jewelry. They each had an armload to deposit on the checkout counter. She had no intention of letting him pay, but he insisted, producing his credit card.

Cara gave in since he clearly wasn't going to back down. "You're very generous, Uncle Neil," she said on the way to the car, each of them lugging large plastic sacks.

"I guess I am techically an uncle, aren't I?" he said.

Like he was "technically" and "temporarily" a husband, Cara assumed he meant. She eased out a sigh, her whole outlook suddenly gloomy. It was so darned hard to stay up beat with the future a big blank.

They'd struck up conversations with space-center employees and with other visitors during the day and Neil had made it a point to inquire about highly recommended restaurants in Huntsville. Therefore Cara wasn't totally unprepared for him to suggest dining out in the city. After they'd stowed their purchases and gotten into the car, he said, "Let's eat dinner before we drive back to Guntersville. Does that plan suit you?"

It didn't suit Cara. Tonight was their last night at the lake cabin, and she would rather eat dinner there, just the two of them. But he obviously preferred not to. "We have those big steaks in the freezer and baking potatoes," she reminded him, in case he'd forgotten.

"I'm not much in the mood for steak, are you? We can leave all our leftover food as a present for the housecleaner."

What he really wasn't in the mood for, Cara suspected, was a romantic evening alone with her. So what was new? It took every bit of acting ability she possessed to say in a cheery tone, "I'll bet we make her day. Or his day. Have you picked out a restaurant?''

Neil glanced at her, and she doubted she'd fooled him. "How about the Golden Dragon?"

Cara knew he wasn't as fond of Chinese food as she was. He was suggesting the Golden Dragon in an effort to please her. "Let's try Luigi's," she said. "It got rave recommendations from everybody who mentioned it."

"There you go, reading my mind." He shook his head with wonder. "You figured out Luigi's was my first choice without my saying a word to tip you off."

She smiled, not denying his accusation. "It wasn't hard. I knew those claims made by the locals about Luigi's serving the best garlic bread in Huntsville were getting your attention. Then somebody mentioned the calamari appetizer."

His sheepish smile made Cara's love spill over. This exchange was typical of others that had lightened the tension during this difficult week, which had proved to be a roller coaster of fun and misery, hope and despair. One moment she could feel completely in tune with him and the next moment feel as though they were on opposite sides of a yawning gulf.

"You don't mind eating Italian?" he asked.

"Me? Mind eating Italian? Is the Pope Catholic?"

If Neil had been avoiding a romantic evening, he'd blundered, Cara reflected a half hour later as she sipped a glass of Chianti and munched on crispy, deep-fried calamari dipped into a marinara sauce to die for. The atmosphere of the restaurant, though not formal, was perfect for romance. The tables, draped in red-and-white checkered tablecloths, were spaced far enough apart for privacy. The lighting was dim, with flickering candles adding their special magic. Music played softly on a sound system.

The other diners were mostly couples and adult foursomes. Cara had glanced around on her way to their corner table and not spotted any small children who might trigger bad memories for Neil. Once she was seated, her attention hadn't strayed away from him. Nor his from her, other than when they placed their order with the waiter, who was friendly enough but not intrusive.

Every course they were served turned out to be outstanding. The garden salad was tossed with a tangy vinaigrette dressing that Cara had to admit was as good as her mother's. The hot-from-the-oven, buttery garlic bread lived up to all the accolades. She and Neil sampled one another's entrées and couldn't decide which was the most delicious, her veal piquante or his linguini with clams in a cream sauce. For dessert they shared a dish of spumoni ice cream and ended with rich, fragrant dark-roast coffee that also didn't disappoint.

"What a feast," Cara declared when they strolled out to her car, arm in arm. "I'll never have a better meal if I live to be a hundred."

"Me neither."

What she'd really meant was "I'll never have a better dining experience,'' and she thought he meant that, too, which added to her happiness.

"Our last night in Alabama,'' Cara said when Neil turned on to the access road to the cabin.

"Our last night,'' he repeated. His voice held a kind of quiet doggedness that implied he would get through this final night, too, somehow.

"Has it been that awful for you?''

"It hasn't been the easiest week of my life. Of your life, either,'' he added.

She sighed. "No. But I'll take away some wonderful memories.''

Neil didn't make any reply. Cara looked at him questioningly, having expected him to say something like "So will I'' or "Same here.'' Wouldn't he take away at least one or two memories he would treasure?

Apparently not. She was crushed. A big lump formed in her throat and tears burned her eyes. A downturn on the emotional roller coaster.

They pulled up in front of the cabin. Neil turned toward her, took her hand and kissed it. "I have a speech,'' he said.

"A speech?''

"Some things I want to say.'' He drew in a breath and released it. "First, thank you for playing straight with me this week. For honoring our bargain about no sex. You could have tipped the scales so easily, like a lot of women would have done just to exercise their power over a man.''

"I was tempted, and not just to exercise my female powers." Cara thought about how she'd fantasized about his coming to her bedroom, about her going to his bedroom, about their making glorious love. "But I wouldn't be able to live with myself if I paid you back for all your generosity by pushing you into doing something you would regret afterwards."

"You're a fine person, Cara. And that's not a recent discovery."

"So are you. And that's not a recent discovery, either."

"I wish the situation with us were different. I wish I could be the right man for you. But I'm not."

The finality and regret in his voice turned Cara's heart to a lump of lead.

"I think you *are* the right man for me, Neil."

"The right man for you, Cara, is a guy who wants a wife, wants a family." And he didn't. How that truth hurt, even though he'd already made his feelings clear on previous occasions. He went on, "You'll look back in a couple of years and, with some perspective, you'll agree with what I'm saying tonight. Trust me." He kissed her hand again and replaced it in her lap.

He'd made his "speech" ever so gently, but the gist of it was "I don't want to be your husband."

What could she say? What could she do to change his mind?

Nothing.

Cara had all she could handle to manage not to break down and cry and make them both feel a hundred times worse than they already felt. She didn't trust herself to speak as she got out of the car, and they went inside the cabin. Neil sank down on the sofa, but Cara didn't join him. "I'm pretty tired," she said. "I believe I'll take a soak in the tub and then go to bed."

"I'm beat, too," he said, concern on his face as he looked at her. "It won't be long before I turn in."

"Good night." She blew him a kiss and turned away quickly toward the bathroom. With water running noisily, she sobbed heartbrokenly as she slowly stripped off her clothes. Of all the emotional lows she'd experienced this week, this low was the worst.

Without admitting as much to herself before now, she'd gambled on the sexual attraction between her and Neil winning out at some point during the week. Naively she'd banked on a happily-ever-after turn of events in which she and Neil would make love rapturously, and he would conquer his fears about risking tragedy again at the same time that he became her lover. He would arrive at the insight that they were meant to be together as man and wife the rest of their lives. The fake honeymoon would have become a real honeymoon. The fake marriage a real marriage.

None of that was going to happen.

And Cara wasn't sure she could bear it not happening. Her despair wasn't just for herself, but for Neil, too. He was denying himself as well as her happiness and fulfillment; dooming himself to loneliness, too.

By the time her bath water had cooled, Cara had

cried herself out and reached a state of sad calm. She heard Neil's footsteps as he retired to his room, heard his door closing.

Earlier she hadn't given any thought to collecting her robe from her bedroom. Her forgetfulness didn't matter now. She wouldn't have to parade past Neil wrapped in a towel. And even if she had done so, he wouldn't have been overcome by desire. It was highly unlikely that they would ever make love, and Cara knew she needed to face up to that reality.

After drying herself off, she draped the damp towel neatly over a bar and gathered up her clothes before making her exit from the bathroom, nude. Neil had left a lamp on. Otherwise she would have had to find her way to her bedroom in the darkness. How like him to be thoughtful, she reflected, breathing out a despondent sigh as she trudged over to turn off the lamp.

Something—Cara wasn't sure what—drew her attention to a set of double windows facing out onto the access road. The curtains weren't drawn, and the glass was an opaque black. It wouldn't be opaque to anyone lurking outside the windows, though. Cara shivered, suddenly uneasy. She walked faster, in a hurry to extinguish the light even while chiding herself, *There's no one out there, silly.*

Just as she reached the lamp table, she heard a noise. A thumping sound that could have been produced by a person or a large animal bumping into the cabin wall. Cara's heart jolted with fright. What if there *was* someone out there, peering at her as she traipsed around, naked as a jaybird?

Was the cabin door locked? She'd been too upset to notice whether Neil had locked it on their return from Huntsville. Should she call out for him just in case there was an intruder? With panicky thoughts flying through her head and her eyes trained on the windows, Cara hugged her clothes against her bare breasts as she leaned down and felt for the lamp switch, located high on the base beneath the lampshade. Her fingers touched the hot light bulb, and she gave out a little shriek and jerked her hand.

The lamp crashed onto the table. But the lampshade must have protected the light bulb. The darn thing kept shining. Before Cara could make another attempt to locate the switch, she heard the door to Neil's bedroom flying open. A different kind of panic took hold.

"Cara, are you all right?" he asked in an alarmed voice. He came toward her, wearing nothing but his boxer shorts. Obviously he'd jumped out of bed.

Realizing that her wad of clothes was sufficient to shield either her bare breasts or her lower torso, not both, Cara collected her wits enough to turn her back to him, facing the blank windows. "I heard a noise outside and got in a big hurry to turn off the lamp. I burned my fingers on the bulb—"

"What kind of noise?"

"A thumping sound. Turn the light off, please. I don't have a stitch of clothes on, as you can see." Her fears about an intruder had dissipated, leaving her embarrassed over creating such a fuss.

He righted the lamp and clicked the switch, plunging the cabin into darkness. "Did you burn yourself badly?" he asked, his tone solicitous.

Cara turned toward him. "Not badly. I'll use some ice later."

"You need to use ice immediately. Come over to the kitchen."

"Neil, really, I can manage."

He ignored her protest and took her arm. Cara balked and didn't move, certain that it wasn't a good idea for them to move around in the dark with her naked and him nearly naked. They should both put on robes. They should turn on lights. But, darn it, her fingers were smarting and there was a certain urgency to administering first aid. Putting aside her qualms, Cara dropped her wad of clothing, figuring she'd need both hands.

Neil steered her over toward the kitchen. During the few seconds en route, Cara's eyes developed enough night vision that she could make out the shape of the dining table and chairs, safely out of their path. He brought her to a standstill near the refrigerator, and she stood waiting while he opened the door to the freezer compartment. A light came on, illuminating a stack of white plastic ice trays and the package of frozen steaks.

"You could just hand me an ice tray," she said.

He took out a tray, but instead of heeding her suggestion, he popped the cubes into a plastic bowl. "Here," he said, pivoting around and extending the bowl.

"Thanks." Cara thrust her fingers into the ice while he continued to hold the bowl for her. "That feels good."

"It should soothe the pain."

The freezer door still hung open, the small appliance bulb beaming out plenty enough light for her to see Neil clearly. And for him to see her clearly. Cara's heartbeat quickened at the intent expression on Neil's face as he looked at her, his gaze dropping to her breasts.

Right on cue, she felt her nipples tingling and tightening into knots in reaction to his male attention. She placed her free arm across her chest. "The cold air from the freezer," she said, offering the best lame excuse she could come up with.

He reached and closed the door, plunging them into pitch blackness again. "Is that better?" he asked. His husky voice had its own stimulating effect.

"Much. Thanks."

Her fingers were starting to ache from contact with the ice. She pulled them out, causing the cubes to rattle noisily. "The ice has done the trick," she said.

"Pain's all gone?" The husky note again, sending shivery excitement through her body.

"Pain's all gone. You can lead me to my bedroom door."

He set the bowl aside. Cara turned away, facing the

direction they needed to go. Instead of stepping to her side and taking her arm again, Neil stayed where he was and placed his hands on either side of her waist. For just a second, Cara wondered if he intended to steer her from behind. Then his arms came around her.

After a second's fleeting surprise, Cara let him draw her against him. He was resting his hips against the counter and took her full weight.

"Neil..." What should have been a protest came out more a yearning invitation.

"I know. I shouldn't do this." He was kissing her neck, her shoulders, his breath hot on her skin. His hands moved up and captured her breasts. Cara uttered a little moan of pure bliss. "Feel good, sweetheart?" he asked.

She was incapable of answering for a moment because he was gently pinching her hard, needy peaks. "Feels incredible," she eventually got out.

He paid her frank, thrilling male compliments about her figure, his hands stroking and caressing and underlining his sincerity. Compliments prefaced by "I love your..." Cara was torn between the selfish desire to give herself over to erotic pleasure, as she had done that other night when he'd attended to her needs, and the determination that she would attend to his needs at least once.

Pleasure nearly got the best of her shortly after he combed his fingers through her dense tangle of curls growing in a triangle and said in a voice resonant with passion, "You're pretty down here, too." He fitted his

hand over her mound, and Cara welcomed the possession with her own murmured words. She welcomed
the delicate exploration of his fingers between her legs.
She cried out with helpless joy when he delved into
her lava-like wetness, but stopped him, clinging to reason.

He straightened up and moved her a few steps forward. After he'd held her in position a second or two
as though making she was balanced on her feet, he
began kissing his way down her back, sending waves
of wild delight through Cara. His breath was hot and
he alternated between nuzzling kisses and open-
mouthed kisses that allowed his tongue to become another stimulus. Simultaneously his hands made the
slow journey down the front of her body, fondling and
inciting.

"Stop," Cara said, when he knelt behind her and
was kissing her buttocks.

He was turning her now, holding her by the hips.
"Turn around and let me—"

"No, Neil. Not here, like this."

"Where, darling?" He sounded drugged and urgent
to continue pleasuring her.

"Let's go to your bedroom. Please?"

He stood and, before she guessed his intention, he'd
picked her up in his arms. "I'm too heavy," she ob-
jected, but obviously she wasn't too heavy. He carried
her easily. Cara wound her arms around his neck and
revelled in his superior strength. At that moment she
wouldn't have traded places with any one of the her-

oines in the romance novels she read. Cara had her own real-life hero, part macho man.

His bedroom door stood open. He turned sideways to enter and carried her over to the bed and laid her on her back. Cara kept her arms around his neck and drew his head down. They hadn't kissed yet, and she was yearning for his mouth on hers.

Neil resisted for a second or two, but he must have been fighting himself, too. "Careful, sweetheart," he said as he gave in. "Help me keep control of myself."

"Don't worry." Cara's aim was to pleasure him, not entice him into unprotected lovemaking that would be unwilling on his part.

The whole concept of any purpose was lost temporarily as their lips met. They kissed with tenderness. With love. With hunger. With deep intimacy, their tongues mating. Neil stretched out beside her and they turned toward each other, pressing their bodies together. The awareness of his aroused manhood as an obstruction between them reminded Cara of her promise she'd made to herself several nights ago.

She raised up and pushed at Neil's shoulder to turn him on his back. He resisted, saying, "No, darling."

"Yes." Cara caressed his chest, slid her palms down over his taut midriff. He made a grab for her hand, but was too late. She was Delilah robbing Samson of his power as she became intimately acquainted with his manhood, stroking, gently capturing him.

Neil groaned and went lax. "Don't," he said without any authority when Cara crouched over him, tugging down his boxer shorts.

"Lie back and close your eyes," she ordered him, her tone loving. She removed the shorts and bent and planted erotic kisses that excited her far more than she'd expected. Turnabout being fair play, she paid him earthy compliments, but confided, "I'm almost glad it's dark. You should see how I'm blushing."

"I could tell." His voice was tender and also rough with pained ecstacy. "Stop right there, sweetheart. I can't stand any more. Cara—"

She didn't stop. He murmured her name and a string of endearments, his elation mixed with entreaty.

Strength must have surged back into his muscles because he reached down and brought her up beside him, the dominant male again. Cara rejoiced in the reversal of roles even as she protested, "But I wanted you to—"

He cut off the explanation with an ardent kiss, and his hands were all over her body, a new urgency in his caresses. The way he touched her made promises he hadn't made before. Cara kissed him back with an ardor that matched his. Her hands stroked him with that same urgency. Dimly she sensed that Neil had crossed over some line of restraint, and there was no backing up. No stopping. Nor did she want to stop.

But she *had* to caution him. Didn't she?

"Neil, are you sure—?"

"Make love with me, Cara."

That was answer enough to allow her to throw caution to the winds, too. Surely he remembered he hadn't come prepared to take precautions and was willing to take the risk. On her part, Cara doubted she could be so lucky as to get pregnant with Neil's baby during one night of unprotected sex.

The thought drifted through her mind and was gone in the next second, along with all rational thinking. Kissing and touching quickly became an unbearable delay, the pleasure taking on a frenzied element.

"Yes," Cara said when Neil positioned himself to couple their bodies. Then he was inside her, and the ecstasy was too sublime for her to withstand. "Wait—" she begged, but Neil was thrusting deeper. Thrusting again. Cara surrendered to the explosive joy and cried out.

In unison with him!

The thrilled realization that he'd reached climax with her made her satisfaction all the sweeter.

"Who said reality never measures up?" To her own ears, Cara sounded as happy and content as she felt, lying close to Neil with his arms around her.

"Measures up to what?"

"Fantasy." His interested silence said, Care to explain? "I've imagined us making love," she confided. "FYI, you're an even better lover than my imagination made you out to be."

"I must have had a little more stamina in your fantasies."

Cara caressed his cheek, amused by his dry remark. "You lasted plenty long enough just now."

He raised up on his elbow and looked down at her. "In this imagined lovemaking, did we make love just once and go to sleep?" His hand fondled her breast. Cara felt the change in his body even as hers stirred to life.

"Who cares what we did in my fantasies?" she replied and drew his head down for a long, slow kiss that finished off her contentment.

Their lovemaking this second time was like the kiss, leisurely, but intense. Loving. Emotional. Neil brought Cara astride him when they'd both reached a fever pitch of need. When she took him inside her, the union was as deep as before, as unbearably sublime. Position obviously had no bearing. Cara lasted slightly longer riding him to climax, maybe fifteen or twenty seconds longer.

Long enough to state rapturously at least half a dozen times, "I love you, Neil!" Long enough for him to tell her more than once, "I love you, Cara!"

Afterwards the conversation was minimal, and Cara fell asleep, a happy, satisfied woman. Life *was* as wonderful as her romance novels.

Or more wonderful.

Chapter Twelve

Neil was feeling great about life in general as he wheeled his bike from the garage. His mom had fixed him pancakes for breakfast. It was summer and the sun was shining. Every day this week he had jobs lined up, still leaving him lots of time to goof around and have fun with his friends. This morning he was headed over to Miss Clara Evanson's place to mow her lawn and weed her flowerbeds. He reckoned he would be through by noon.

By the time school started in the fall, he hoped to have enough money saved up to buy a used car. Or enough with the matching money his dad would put up. Neil had his eye on the blue Chevy parked on a used-car lot downtown. It had sat there for weeks, and *he had his fingers crossed that it didn't get sold. The spots of rust and the dents didn't bother him. He could do the bodywork himself, tune up the engine.*

Neil hopped on his bike and coasted down the sloping driveway to the street, where he braked to let a big eighteen-wheeler go rumbling past. An eighteen-wheeler on his street? Where the heck was that monster going in a residential neighborhood? And the driver was speeding, too. Didn't he see the signs that said Slow, Children At Play?

Two blocks away little Cara LaCroix was probably pedalling her tricycle on the edge of the street in front of her house. Neil always took that route if it wasn't too much out of his way because he knew she kept a watch out for him. Her mother had told his mother, who'd told him. Her cute face would light up when she spotted him, and she'd wave and command him to stop and talk to her. If he wasn't in too much of a hurry, he would. It amused him that she was such a bright, bossy little girl.

Alarmed for the little girl's safety, Neil followed the eighteen-wheeler, pedalling hard. The darned truck kept accelerating and getting farther ahead. Neil pumped his legs faster and faster, but he couldn't gain any ground. Between panic and exertion, his heart was pounding in his chest. His breath was coming in gasps.

Mothers appeared in doorways. Neil saw their faces in his peripheral vision and realized they were shouting out warnings, voicing that same fear that gripped him. But he couldn't hear what they were saying because of the deafening roar of the eighteen-wheeler's engine.

Up ahead was Cara's block. Dear God, she was riding her tricycle on the street, not along the edge but out in the middle! Neil pedaled faster than it was humanly possible, but the truck pulled even farther ahead of him.

"Cara, get out of the street!" he yelled so loudly that his vocal cords hurt. At the risk of crashing his bike, he waved both arms wildly, screaming the warning again and again.

Finally she looked around and saw him. She also must have seen the truck, but she didn't seem to pay any attention to it. Smiling happily, she waved at Neil and turned her bicycle up the street, heading straight into the path of the eighteen-wheeler.

In seconds she would be killed! And Neil was powerless to do anything!

"God, no..."

"Neil, wake up!"

Cara's voice roused him from the nightmare. Relief flooded Neil, flushing away the terror. "You're grown up," he murmured. "You're safe."

"As safe as I could ever be. I'm right here in bed with you."

In bed with him? With both of them naked? "Cara, what's—?" Memory cleared away Neil's confusion and remorse hit him. Dear God, what had he done?

How could he have been so irresponsible as to let last night happen?

"Are you okay?" she asked, hugging him.

"I'm fine. Just a bad dream. Let's get some more sleep," he said, wide awake. After she'd fallen asleep, Neil lay listening to the sound of her even breathing, dreading tomorrow.

When Cara awoke the next morning, she was alone in Neil's bed. She raised her head and listened, but didn't hear a sound out in the cabin. The door to the bedroom was ajar.

"Neil?" she said.

No answer.

Cara tried to dismiss her feeling of foreboding. Neil might be out on the porch enjoying the morning and waiting eagerly for her to join him. There was no reason to be fearful. After they'd made love last night, he hadn't expressed any regret.

Of course, they really hadn't talked. She'd been utterly contented and physically satisfied and had gone out like a light. Some time before daylight he'd had a nightmare, she suddenly remembered.

Please, let him be glad today, Cara prayed, getting out of bed and wrapping the top sheet like a toga.

No coffee aroma greeted her as she emerged from the bedroom, but then he hadn't brewed coffee *every* morning during the week. "Neil?" she said again, and again no answer.

Cara advanced into the cabin far enough to peer out

the windows giving her a view of the back porch. He wasn't out on the porch. Then she saw him on their small private pier. Something about his posture as he stood with his hands in his pockets, gazing out at the lake, made Cara's heart sink. Even with his back to her, she could tell his thoughts probably weren't happy thoughts.

"Oh, darn," she muttered in dismay. "I hope he's not rehearsing another speech." A speech she wouldn't want to hear about last night's being a big mistake.

Cara started a pot of coffee brewing before she headed to her bedroom to throw on some clothes. Dark liquid was still dripping into the carafe of the coffee-maker a few minutes later when she took a couple of mugs from a cabinet shelf, but Cara filled the mugs quickly anyway and fixed Neil's coffee the way he usually drank it, black with one spoon of sugar.

A glass holding a residue of orange juice sat on the small table on the porch. Evidently Neil had spent some time sitting on the porch, long enough to drink the glass of orange juice, Cara deduced.

"Good morning," she called cheerfully, approaching the dock with a mug in each hand.

Neil turned around. His expression was as somber as she'd feared. "Hi," he said.

"How long have you been up?" she asked.

"Since it got full daylight. I didn't go back to sleep after I had the nightmare."

"I'm sorry. I wish you'd woken me up."

"There was no point in disturbing your sleep." He took the mug she handed him. "Thanks."

"In exchange for this, do I get a good-morning kiss?"

He gave her a chaste kiss on the mouth.

"We're back to good buddies, I take it." Cara sighed. Despite having sized up the situation, she was still sick with disappointment.

"Cara, last night—"

She cut in. "I can fill in the blanks for myself, Neil. You don't have to spell it out for me that last night didn't change anything for you."

"It was the most foolhardy behavior of my entire life. I just pray I didn't get you pregnant. When will we know?"

Cara did some calculation. "About three weeks from now. I had just had my period before the wedding."

"Three weeks." He sounded as though it would be an eternity for him while he sweated out the wait.

"I doubt we have anything to worry about. Excuse me. I need to go and pack my things." Cara turned away and started walking toward the cabin, incapable of carrying on further discussion about whether she might be pregnant. Or about anything right now. How was it possible, she wondered, to feel as close to Neil as she'd felt last night when they'd made love and then to feel this distant? To be on top of the world and then hours later to be this miserable?

Life wasn't like a romance novel at all. Not her life,

anyway. And Cara was tired of the emotional roller coaster.

"Goodbye, little cabin," Cara said as she got into the car. Her voice was sad.

Neil bit back the words, *I'm sorry.* Another apology wouldn't change a damn thing. What they both had to do now was put their honeymoon week behind them and go on.

"Tell me about your nightmare," she said when they'd turned onto the highway. "When I woke you up, you seemed relieved that I was alive and well. So I gather I was in your dream."

"You were." He recounted the nightmare, reliving some of the same terror and helplessness when he came to the last part, where the eighteen-wheeler was bearing down on a preschool Cara.

"How odd that the differences in our ages is all wrong," she said. "I'm only five years younger than you. So I would have been eleven if you were sixteen. I wouldn't have been riding a tricycle. If I had been that small and was playing on the street, Nonna would have been keeping a close eye on me. She would have snatched me up and told that truck driver off."

The image made Neil smile. "She would have read him the riot act, wouldn't she?" He went on, "The age disparity struck me as odd, too. But dreams aren't logical. A psychiatrist could probably analyze this one pretty easily."

"You've analyzed it yourself," she guessed.

"Some elements are obvious. The fact that I'm happy at the beginning and the world is a great place. Without any warning, a tragic situation develops and there's nothing I can do to prevent it. I'm a helpless onlooker."

"You were out of town when Lisa and Chris were in the accident that killed them, weren't you?"

He followed her thought: He hadn't witnessed the fatal accident. "Yes, I'd left them that morning." Instinctively Neil started to shut down the memory, and then he let himself recall the details. "Lisa had fixed us a big breakfast."

"Not pancakes?"

"No. A Mexican omelet, she called it. With sautéed onions and peppers and grated cheese." His stomach reacted with nausea. He hadn't eaten any kind of omelet since that last meal with his family. "She fixed Chris a scrambled egg, but he was too excited to eat."

When he didn't continue, Cara touched his arm gently and prompted, "Why was he so excited?"

Neil went on, "Lisa was ready to have another baby, and I was all for it, too. We wanted to lay the groundwork with Chris, so we asked him during breakfast how he would like a little brother or sister. He wanted to go and get one or the other—he didn't care which—immediately."

"How sweet."

"After breakfast I kissed them both and hugged them and told them goodbye. Drove away in my company car, on top of the world."

"Oh, Neil, no wonder you're afraid to be happy." She swiped at tears of sadness trickling down her cheeks.

"Please don't cry."

"I won't. Those two tears just spilled out."

He reached over and squeezed her hand. "I'm not unhappy. Or I haven't been for the last year anyway. You know that from being around me at work." As to what state he would be in when this fake marriage ended, Neil could only hope for the best. The important thing was seeing that she survived intact and could go on about her life, a whole, happy person. To that end he had to make sure there wasn't a repeat of last night. With or without birth control.

Neil was praying he'd gotten by with his recklessness last night and Cara wasn't sitting next to him, pregnant. It had taken several months of frequent lovemaking for Lisa to conceive, and among their circle of friends the norm had been more like six months to a year for conception. Still, Neil would be greatly relieved when the three weeks had gone past and Cara got her period.

"Did you know there *was* an incident involving an eighteen-wheeler in our neighborhood one year?" she asked, breaking into his somber thoughts. "I'm fairly certain it happened after you'd moved away to Memphis. The truck driver was sleep-deprived and made some wrong turns, ending up on Azalea, which, of course, is a dead-end street. He had to back out and in the process wiped out some mailboxes and totalled a tricycle or two parked on the ends of driveways. The police came and wrote him a ticket. A news photographer showed up and took pictures. The story was on the front page of the Hammond newspaper.''

"I'll bet my mother clipped out that article and sent it to me." The incident had a ring of familiarity. He snapped his fingers. "Miss Clara Evanson lived on Azalea, didn't she?"

"She still does. She buys Natural Beauty products from Natalie and calls my mother to place her order.''

"Miss Evanson must be pushing ninety. I'm glad to hear she's still active.''

"Someone else you knew lived on Azalea, too. Mary Jane Simmons. She chased you all through high school, remember?''

Neil glanced over at her, his eyebrows raised at her tone. "You didn't like Mary Jane?"

Cara made a face. "I was jealous of her. Along with all the other girls you dated.''

"*All* the other girls? I didn't date that many girls.''

"Oh, yes, you did. Want me to list them for you?" She did, ticking the names off on her fingers.

Neil was amused, not to mention amazed at her recall. The subject of his past girlfriends didn't much interest him, but he was glad to talk about anything that would lighten the atmosphere and get his mind and hers off last night and the possible repercussions.

"One of these days I'm going to be the first one out of bed,'' Cara said, yawning as she headed for the coffeemaker.

"Did you sleep well?" he asked, turning a page of the section of newspaper he had open before him on the table in his kitchen.

"Like a log. I must have fallen asleep as soon as my head touched the pillow." Which rather surprised her, since last night had been her first night to sleep in Neil's house. She'd figured she might lie awake for hours, tossing and turning.

"The bed is comfortable then?"

"Very comfortable."

"Good."

She sat across from him and he slid the rest of the Saturday newspaper closer to her. Cara located the Living section and began reading the lead article, sipping her coffee.

A half hour later, Neil asked, "Would you like to go out for breakfast?"

"Not really," she replied honestly. "Would you?"

"No. I've had my quota of cholesterol."

"Plus we'd be sure to run into people we know, and I'm not in much of a social mood."

"Me either."

"Why don't I make a quick run to the nearest convenience store and buy some milk and bread? And anything else we need for a light breakfast." Cara was getting up as she spoke, already mentally making a beeline to her bedroom to get dressed.

"I've already gone."

"You have?" He was rising to his feet. "Sit back down," she said. "I'll fix you whatever you want."

"Thanks, but I can fix my own."

Cara wanted to wage more protest, but he obviously meant to wait on himself.

"I bought peanut butter and yogurt," he said. "I hope I got a flavor you like."

The breakfast food she had a yen for was buttered toast, but when Cara opened the refrigerator and saw a dozen individual-serving containers of yogurt, she selected one and ate the yogurt with her toast. Neil ate a bowl of cereal with sliced banana.

After they'd finished, Cara got up with the intention of loading the few dishes into the dishwasher and tidying up the kitchen. "Let me handle this," she said as he got to his feet. "There isn't much to do."

He took no heed and shared the minor cleanup. On the one hand, Cara appreciated his not assuming she would take over housewifely chores and wait on him hand and foot, but she had a nagging suspicion there was more to his behavior than being considerate.

Did he want to keep her a guest in his house?

"Don't feel like you have to keep me company today," he said when they'd finished.

"Great minds. I was about to say the same thing to you," Cara replied. "Feel free to do whatever you feel like doing. I plan to catch up with laundry."

"In that case, I think I'll fool around out in the garage for a while."

Cara could sense that he welcomed some time to himself and empathized. The so-called honeymoon had been a strain on both of them, but on him more so than her. She didn't require a lot of privacy, perhaps because she'd grown up in a large family. Understanding all that, she still felt a twinge of hurt when Neil didn't waste a second escaping to the garage.

Turning her attention to her own agenda, Cara went to her room and shed the pink-and-white robe she'd slipped on earlier before joining Neil in the kitchen. After she'd gotten dressed in shorts and a sleeveless blouse suitable for working around the house, she made up her bed, finished unpacking her suitcases and collected her soiled clothes.

In the laundry room she saw that Neil had already deposited his soiled clothing into a wire basket. Good, she thought. Now she wouldn't have to stick her head through the door leading into the garage and ask him if he minded her getting his laundry from his bedroom.

Neil had turned on his boom box, and Cara could hear the music. She hummed along to the country and western tune as she sorted garments into piles. Jeans. Dark colors. Light colors. White.

The first load had just begun its washing cycle when the door opened and Neil asked, "Did you find everything you need?"

"Yes, I did. We even buy the same brand of laundry detergent."

He was gazing at the piles of garments, frowning. "You're not washing my clothes, are you?"

"Do you mind?"

"I'm used to doing my own laundry, Cara. I certainly don't expect you to do it."

"It's almost as easy to wash everything while I'm at it."

"You're not the housekeeper or the maid. Just toss my clothes back into the basket." He pulled the door closed and then opened it again long enough to tell her, "I have an iron and an ironing board, if you need to use them. They're in that locker in the corner."

"Thanks."

Cara was crushed. He hadn't answered her question directly when she'd asked, "Do you mind?" But obviously he did mind. He didn't want her to assume any housewifely chores. Why? Because he was afraid she might start thinking she really was his wife?

"You will *not* cry, Cara LaCroix," she muttered fiercely to herself as she did Neil's bidding and replaced his clothes in the basket, but tears splashed on several garments, forming wet spots.

She was putting away the ironing board and iron when Neil came back into the house a couple of hours later. He smelled faintly of gasoline.

"All done?" he asked.

"All done."

He stripped off his T-shirt and dropped it into the washing machine after he'd checked to make sure the machine was empty. "Let's go out and have some lunch."

"Okay. I'll go change."

"Give me fifteen minutes to shower."

"Take as long as you need." Cara was expecting him to follow behind her. When he didn't, she paused at the doorway and looked back. He'd kicked off his ratty athletic shoes and was shucking his jeans.

"Caught me in the act," he said with a sheepish grin. He dropped the jeans into the washing machine and stood there in his boxer shorts.

She smiled at him, enjoying her view. Her pique had melted away and, along with it, her defenses. "Is that what you usually do when you come in from the garage? Strip down to your drawers?"

"I usually take them off, too."

"Don't let me change your routine." Pulses fluttering, Cara hurried on to her bedroom. Darn, she wished she could leave the door open so she could see him passing by.

At the restaurant where they ate lunch, they encountered friends and acquaintances, as was almost inevitable wherever they went in the town of Hammond. They responded to well-meaning comments like, "Here are the lovebirds, back from their honeymoon!" Cara played her role of new wife and felt like a terrible phony.

"I hate this, don't you?" she said to Neil in a low voice after a couple who were longtime friends of his parents had come by their table to say hello. "Being off among strangers was a lot easier, in retrospect."

"We're an item, but we won't be for long." He squeezed her hand reassuringly.

"Tomorrow we go back to work. Jimmy and Peewee and Allison and Mary Ann will be watching us like hawks, expecting us to act like newlyweds. I'm sure you must be dreading it.'' She gazed at him questioningly when he shrugged. ''Aren't you?''

''The public spotlight isn't so bad for me.''

Relative to what? Cara didn't ask because she knew the answer. For him to spell it out would only be more depressing. What he found difficult was having Cara as his housemate and dealing with their time together without anyone else around. This morning being an example.

''Well, look who's back in town! Mr. and Mrs. Neil Griffin!''

Cara plastered a smile on her face as she responded to another person who'd detoured by their table to say hello.

When they were alone again, Cara turned to Neil and asked, ''Did you accomplish a lot this morning, working on your car you're fixing up?''

''I tinkered with the carburetor. I'm not in a hurry to restore the car,'' he explained. ''I'll probably sell it when I'm done and start on another one. It's just pastime.''

But hadn't seemed like pastime today. The two hours out in the garage had seemed more like six hours as he tried in vain to focus on his task, battling the urge to go inside and talk to her, be with her. Battling less platonic urges, too. Making love to her night before last had only made him want her more.

And love her more.

If Cara could be happy and satisfied as his wife and forego being a mother, Neil might find the courage to become a real husband to her. But she wouldn't be happy and satisfied.

Neil just didn't have it in him to become a husband and father again. He couldn't live with that much fear and anxiety.

"Do you need to do any shopping at the mall?" he asked later when they were in the car.

"Do you?" she replied.

"I could use some new athletic shoes."

"Why don't we go to the mall then?"

"You don't mind?"

"Not at all."

They ran into more people they knew, including a former high-school classmate of Cara's who was pushing her baby in a stroller. Neil watched with a bleak sensation as Cara addressed the infant in baby talk and went into raptures when she coaxed a smile.

The episode reinforced what he already knew. Marriage to him wouldn't be enough. Nature had instilled in her the need to be a mother.

There was a slim possibility she might be pregnant. With his child. What if she were? Neil shied away from the question. He was ninety-nine-percent sure he wouldn't have to answer it.

Chapter Thirteen

Music disturbed Cara's sound sleep. Music from her radio on the bedside table. She opened her eyes wide enough to peek at the radio's clock face and let her heavy lids drop. A moment later she looked at the clock again and sat up in bed, nonplussed.

Not waking up when the radio came on was starting to become a habit. What was her problem lately? She'd never slept quite this soundly, which she found amazing considering how nerve-wracking the past two weeks had been. Post-honeymoon weeks. When she laid her head on the pillow in Neil's guest room, she zonked out.

He obviously wasn't so lucky. His lack of restful sleep showed enough to make him the target of ribald teasing at the store, the assumption being that Neil was overly ardent as a bridegroom. Nothing was further from the truth, of course. He'd only lost his control that once, their last evening at the lake cabin.

It was well within Cara's power to make him lose it again, an intuition that put her under increasing strain as time went on. She would catch him looking at her with sexual longing that sparked her own desire. The tension was so bad that they didn't kiss or hug when they were alone. Only in public when it was safe to be affectionate.

Cara sighed as she climbed out of bed. Maybe I'm sleeping as an escape, she reflected.

Conscious that she was running behind schedule, she didn't bother with putting on her robe. The guest bathroom was just down the hall. Neil would be in the kitchen, out of sight, showered and dressed. Visualizing him brought a smile to Cara's face and a rush of love.

But also a pang of sadness. She was losing hope, day by day, preparing herself for the inevitable. There *would* be a divorce eventually.

Out in the hallway, she noticed that the door to Neil's bedroom was closed. Normally it stood open in the morning when she made her trek to the bathroom. Also, there was usually a coffee aroma wafting from the kitchen.

Had he overslept, too?

Cara changed directions and walked barefoot toward the kitchen. From the doorway she noted that no lights were on. The coffee carafe sat empty. The newspaper hadn't been brought inside and must still be out on the driveway.

Now faintly worried that Neil might have fallen ill, she retraced her route and headed to the master bedroom at the end of the hallway. After tapping lightly and speaking his name, she cocked her head and listened for an answer.

Silence.

He might be in the shower. Cara grasped the doorknob, reasoning that she should be able to hear the water running if she opened the door. Instead she heard the sound of deep, slow breathing.

Neil *was* still asleep.

Cara eased the door farther open and gazed at him, concern and love mingling in a single strong, tender emotion. Poor guy. He'd had another bad night. His tangled, rumpled bedding told the story of tossing and turning. He lay on his stomach, his cheek buried in a feather pillow that had taken some pummeling.

On the carpet lay a litter of magazines. Had he read all those and tossed them there?

I'll just let him sleep, Cara thought. With that decision made, she couldn't seem to tear herself away. Looking at him gave her such feminine pleasure. His bare back and shoulders and arms were exposed and so was one long leg.

"Cara, darling, please..."

At the sound of his voice, Cara jumped with surprise. He'd spoken in his sleep. Apparently he was dreaming about her. "Please what?" she asked softly. A powerful urge to be nearer to him drew her over to the bed.

"Please…" he said again.

"Anything, my love." She sat on the edge of the mattress and carefully placed her hand on his back, needing to touch him.

He drew in a deep breath and remained soundly asleep. Cara gently massaged the spot her hand covered, his skin warm and vital to the touch. He made a sound in his throat and murmured, "Yes, darling."

She brought her other hand into play, indulging herself in the pleasure of touching him while she lavished love with her palms and the pads of her fingers. Emboldened after she had attended to his entire back and shoulders, Cara bent and kissed him.

A quiver went through his body, and he raised his head. Looked around at her. "Cara." His drowsy voice held the same wonder and love and male desire she saw on his face.

Her apology died on her lips as he turned over onto his side with a lithe twist of his long body and reached for her. The next thing Cara knew she was stretched out next to him, transported to heaven in his arms.

Just a few moments of this bliss and she would get up, she told herself. The resolve vanished before the alloted moments had passed. Neil's embrace loosened, but only to allow his hands the freedom to slip beneath her oversize T-shirt. Cara's moan of pleasure was trapped in her throat as his mouth found hers.

Maybe if there had been any conversation, they might have contained the pent-up sexual need that had been building, but Neil spoke only with his hungry kisses and his urgent caresses, his message: I'll die if I don't make love to you. Cara answered in kind, sending the message back to him.

Briefly, she came to her senses when Neil stripped off her T-shirt. "What about birth control?" she asked.

"I'm prepared," was all he said, lowering his head to plant hot kisses on her breasts. The frenzied pace became more frenzied until there was finally conversation of the most basic kind expressing the need for haste.

Neil jerked open a drawer in his bedside table, rummaged inside. Cara tore open the packet, helped him, guided him. At long last, he thrust inside her. An all-encompassing joy exploded into ecstasy. Exulting in the union of their bodies, the fusion of their love, Cara rode the crest with him. His climax triggered her own tumultuous release.

"You were dreaming about me?"

"A sexy dream. I opened my eyes, and there you were."

Cara planted a kiss on his shoulder, and he rewarded her by hugging her closer.

"I overslept again this morning. When I got up, I discovered you'd overslept, too," she explained.

"My alarm went off. I vaguely remember turning it off. I was going to catch another fifteen minutes."

"You were late getting to sleep?"

"The last time I looked at the clock, it was 4:00 a.m."

Cara gathered her courage. "This no-sex arrangement hasn't worked, Neil. We're too attracted to each other."

"It's been hell," he said with feeling.

"Have you given any thought to making ours a real marriage?"

"What do you think keeps me up until 4:00 a.m? Of course I think about it. And I keep coming to the same conclusion: I can't offer you what you want. Not the whole package."

"Meaning?"

"Children."

Cara absorbed what he seemed to be telling her. She could have him as her husband if she were willing to give up motherhood. He would take the risk of losing another wife, but not losing another family. "Of course, I'll take the partial package, Neil, if my alternative is a divorce later on."

"Imagine what being childless would be like, Cara. I saw your face a couple of weeks ago when we ran into your former classmate and her baby. You would have taken that baby home with you."

"Sure, I love babies. But if I have to choose between being your wife without babies and some other man's wife with babies, I'll pick you every time. Are you giving me that choice?'' she asked, her voice hopeful.

''Yes, but I want you to take more time and think about what you would be giving up.'' He hesitated, and when he continued, his tone was even more sober. ''There wouldn't be a slipup. I would have to make sure of that.''

In other words he wouldn't rely on condoms or other methods of birth control that weren't foolproof. He would take the surgical measure—a vasectomy.

''The Pill is almost foolproof,'' she protested, appalled.

He didn't say anything, and he didn't need to. Cara had just realized she was holding out the hope he'd change his mind and eventually want children. And he'd known that, because he understood her better than anyone else did.

Would she be truly happy never experiencing motherhood? No, Cara doubted she would. On the other hand, she loved Neil and wanted so much to be his real wife. She couldn't fathom being truly happy living apart from him, not now.

What was Cara to do? She seemed to be in a no-win situation.

''I guess we're back to the no-sex rule while I'm making up my mind,'' she said, her tone despondent.

''Don't you think that's wise?'' He didn't sound any happier than she did.

She sighed, forced to admit it *was* wise, though no easier than it ever had been.

* * *

"Look at you! Aren't you pretty as a picture with that blush in your cheeks?" declared Sophia. She gave Cara's right cheek a gentle pinch.

"You're looking pretty yourself in that red dress, Nonna." Cara hugged her grandmother. Rose LaCroix was standing by, smiling and waiting her turn. "So do you, Mamma," Cara said, giving her mother a hug, too.

"Lunch is ready, and the table's all set," Rose said. "Your daddy made himself scarce so we could have a hen party. Have you talked to Natalie lately?"

"Not in the last couple of days. What's up with her?"

Sophia jumped in, "She's got a terrible case of poison ivy. Poor thing, she's taking shots."

"I keep telling her not to do yard work, but Natalie was always hardheaded," Rose said.

Cara managed to get in a few words of commiseration on her oldest sister's behalf as she sat down to an ample lunch with her mother and grandmother. "This is such a treat," she declared at one point, with complete sincerity.

On the way to the LaCroix home, Cara had psyched herself up for the lunch date, not wanting Sophia and Rose to suspect that all wasn't well in her life, but pleasure in the visit was doing the trick. She'd needed the reminder that she had a great deal to be thankful for, despite her current dilemma. Her family was a major blessing.

"Have some more shrimp-and-pasta salad," Rose urged after Cara had eaten all the food on her plate. Sophia was holding out a basket of warm homemade rolls.

Cara refused the salad but couldn't resist taking another roll. "All of a sudden I seem to have developed this appetite for bread," she remarked. "Every morning I'm making myself toast."

"You never particularly liked toast," said her mother.

"Now I do."

Rose and Sophia exchanged glances. Big smiles spread across their faces. Cara looked from one to the other in puzzlement.

"She's pregnant," they declared in unison.

"Because I started eating toast? Don't be silly."

"Any other changes in your eating habits?" Rose asked.

Cara thought. "I've lost my taste for certain flavors of yogurt." Flavors that had been her favorites, oddly enough. "But I haven't craved dill pickles or ice cream."

Sophia batted the air with her hand. "Neither did I when I was pregnant. Neither did Rose. It's all individual. I craved apples, of all things. Normally, apples didn't appeal to me at all."

"I craved popcorn," Rose recalled, rolling her eyes.

They quizzed Cara and she told them truthfully that she hadn't missed a period yet. She didn't disclose that her period should be starting in a day or two. By tomorrow or the next day, if Cara wasn't pregnant, she should begin to feel achy and heavy in her abdomen.

She probably *wasn't* pregnant.

But what if she was? The possibility was both thrilling and frightening. Cara had never had such mixed feelings about anything. She couldn't say to herself "I hope I'm pregnant" or "I hope I'm not pregnant."

If Neil's baby wasn't growing inside her now, she would have lost her only chance to be the mother of his child. Their child. If his baby *was* growing inside her, she would have to deal with telling him that his worst fear had come true.

"I'm off to the post office. And a few other places," Cara said. She smiled, hoping she didn't look as guilty as she felt.

"Take the rest of the afternoon off, why don't you?" Neil kissed her lightly on the mouth. "Allison can handle things in the office."

"Thanks. I might do that."

Cara fled the store. After she'd completed her errands in record time, she drove to Ponchatoula, a neighboring town, and pulled into a strip shopping center on the outskirts. Her destination was a pharmacy located next to a supermarket. So far, so good, she thought, hurrying inside the pharmacy. With any luck she would find what she needed, buy it and be on her way back to Hammond without being seen or recognized.

A young male employee who was stocking shelves

offered his assistance, but Cara politely refused. It was silly of her, she knew, to be rather embarrassed. After walking up and down several aisles, she succeeded in her search and was making her selection when a female voice spoke her name.

"Cara. I thought that was you."

In her surprise, Cara jerked her hand, and half a dozen boxes toppled to the floor. Ignoring the mess she'd made and trying desperately not to give the impression she'd been caught doing something illegal, Cara took a hasty step toward the woman bearing down upon her. "Hi there, Joan. How are you?"

Of all the rotten luck, she'd run smack dab into Allison Pendergast's sister!

"Fine. What brings you to Ponchatoula?"

"I had some business to attend to."

"Let me help you pick those up." Joan was eyeing the pregnancy kits on the floor.

"Don't bother. I'll pick them up." Cara stood her ground, so that the other woman had to edge past her.

"That brand is very reliable. I know because I tested positive both times I was pregnant."

"A friend of mine who couldn't get out to shop asked me to buy one for her. I'll pass along what you said."

"Oh. I was hoping you were buying it for yourself. Allison would be thrilled over the news that you and Neil were starting your family. She thinks you'll make the world's greatest mother. Well, it was nice talking to you."

"Same here."

Cara made a dismayed face at Joan's back and bent to retrieve the scattered boxes. The other woman hadn't believed Cara's lame story about buying the kit for a friend. The cat was out of the bag, darn it. By the time Cara arrived back in Hammond, Joan would have phoned Allison at the store, and Cara wouldn't put it past her co-worker to blab to Neil.

So far he hadn't asked Cara if she'd gotten her period. Maybe he simply assumed she had, since she hadn't told him otherwise. Cara had decided to wait and determine whether she was pregnant or simply experiencing a new irregularity in her menstrual cycle before she raised an alarm. Using a pregnancy kit was one step in figuring out what was what. The next step would have been visiting a gynecologist on the sly. But running into Joan today had probably wrecked any chances of keeping Neil in the dark a week or two longer, Cara reflected with a sigh as she headed to the checkout counter with two kits by different manufacturers. She'd decided to be doubly sure.

It hadn't been Cara's plan to sneak to Ponchatoula, purchase a couple of pregnancy kits and rush straight home to do the home tests. Dread at what she might find out had blocked a sense of urgency. She'd figured she could use the kits later that night after she'd said good-night to Neil and retired to her bedroom.

Back in her car, Cara discovered she'd undergone a change in attitude now that she had the home test kits in her possession. There *was* a sense of urgency now, and it didn't arise just from encountering Joan.

Cara wanted to know. For herself.

The dread was different suddenly, too. Her worst fear, she realized, was a negative test result.

Forty minutes later Cara gazed in wonderment at the two test indicators on her bathroom counter, one a slender wand and the other a small square box. She'd read the instructions carefully for each test, followed the two different procedures for urine analysis just as carefully.

Both tests had read positive.

I'm pregnant with Neil's baby! Cara marveled.

She was putting together a lasagne dish for supper and humming with giddy joy when she heard Neil's truck in the driveway. Surely he would be glad despite all he'd said about no children, Cara thought. A baby was *such* a miracle.

"Something sure smells delicious," he said, entering the kitchen. "But weren't we eating out tonight?"

"I decided to cook since I had the afternoon off." Cara smiled at him. After she'd resumed sprinkling coarsely grated cheese, she was aware of his close scrutiny.

"The break certainly did you good," he remarked. "According to Allison, her sister Joan saw you over in Ponchatoula." His tone was only mildly curious, indicating he hadn't gotten a full report.

"That's the thing about small towns. Somebody always recognizes you." Cara slid the lasagne into the oven. "Let's have a beer." Immediately she revised the suggestion, "Or you have a beer. I'll have a glass of apple juice."

He raised his eyebrows slightly. "Apple juice?"

"I'm on a health kick," she explained, walking over to the refrigerator.

Having opened a bottle of beer for him and poured herself apple juice, she led the way into the living room. Before Neil could sit in his leather recliner, Cara linked her arm in his and said, "Sit by me on the sofa. Please."

He hesitated, but did as she requested. "Is there some mystery you're about to reveal?" he asked. "Allison kept making cryptic remarks and smirking like the cat who'd swallowed the canary after she heard about your being in Ponchatoula. My birthday isn't coming up," he added.

Cara sipped her juice, fortifying herself, then set the glass down. "I ran into Joan in a pharmacy. I was shopping in the department with pregnancy kits."

"Why—" He broke off, obviously stunned as comprehension hit him. "God, don't tell me—" He gazed at her beseechingly.

She nodded. Her giddy joy died.

Neil was clutching the bottle of beer with both hands, his knuckles showing white. He tipped his head back, his eyes squeezed closed. He opened them and Cara winced at his haggard expression. It was the expression of a man who was trapped in a nightmare.

"You haven't been to a doctor?" he asked.

"No, not yet."

"Those pregnancy kits aren't one hundred per cent reliable. Peewee's wife tested positive last year, and she wasn't pregnant, remember? Sometime they leave the kits on the shelf too long."

"I looked at the expiration dates. And I used two different kits."

"You haven't had symptoms, have you? Morning sickness?"

Cara shook her head. She laid both hands protectively over her abdomen. "But I'm in tune with my body enough to know something's different. I'll go to my gynecologist and make certain."

"Pray those kits are wrong, Cara."

"I can't send up that prayer." She touched his arm, wanting to comfort and reassure him. "It won't be the end of the world. I'll raise the baby myself. You don't have to be involved."

"What do you mean you'll raise it yourself? We'll have to stay married now."

"We don't have to stay married. And we won't." Cara spoke with sadness and finality. "Not unless you can honestly say to me, 'I want this child we're bringing into the world.'"

"You know I can't say that."

His anguished words stirred her love and compassion, but also extinguished any ember of hope.

Chapter Fourteen

"My mother sent you some lunch." Cara indicated the flat round plastic container she carried. "Come into the lounge and I'll reheat it in the microwave for you."

Neil followed her. He wasn't hungry. These days he had to force food down, but it was an excuse to spend thirty minutes with her.

"Here. Let me," he said when they'd entered the employees' lounge. He held out his hand for the container.

"I'll do it. You sit down."

Neil did as he was told, taking a chair that allowed him to watch her. Three-and-a-half-months pregnant, she wore a pink maternity dress that, like everything she wore, was extremely becoming. She'd been pretty before, but pregnancy had given her a radiant beauty. He couldn't get enough of looking at her even though his pleasure was spoiled by a whole mix of confused emotions.

"How was Sophia feeling today?" he inquired, mindful that Cara had returned from a daily visit to her grandmother, whose health was deteriorating as she lost her battle with cancer. She was now under hospice care.

"Nonna was in good spirits, as always. She's convinced my baby is a girl."

Neil didn't remark on Cara's use of the pronoun *my* instead of *our*. He knew there was no jab intended. She wasn't bitter or resentful toward him, which only made him feel worse about letting her down. He'd begun seeing a therapist, but didn't seem to be making any headway in dealing with his negative feelings about becoming a father again.

Cara served him, placing two paper plates on the table, one with green salad and the other heaped with spaghetti and meatballs. "Doesn't this look good?" she said.

In lieu of lying, Neil responded, "Hmm. Thanks." He accepted a fork and paper napkin and speared some salad. "How did Sophia predict the sex of the baby?" *The* was always his choice of pronoun for their unborn child.

Cara sat down across from him. "She had a wonderful dream in which she held her in her arms and rocked her in the old family rocking chair. I hope Nonna's right and I have a little girl.''

''You want a daughter so you can name her after your grandmother?'' he guessed, his tone gentle.

She nodded and smiled a sad smile. ''If that's okay with you.''

''Of course, it's okay with me. Not that I'm indifferent,'' he added quickly, realizing his words could be interpreted as indifference.

''I understand what you meant,'' she said, her expression loving but also resigned. ''Eat your lunch.''

Neil applied himself to chewing and swallowing while she chatted with him about various subjects. Gradually the intuition grew that she was waiting until he'd finished eating to tell him something. Something that might kill his appetite, obviously.

''Rose was too generous with her portions. I can't hold all this,'' he said, putting his fork down.

''Can I have a sip?'' She reached for his can of cola and drew her hand back. ''The caffeine. I forgot.''

He got up and went to the refrigerator and took out a small can of orange juice. After opening it and giving it to her, he sat down again and asked, ''What's on your mind?''

''Was I that obvious?''

''For you to almost slip up and take a swallow of a beverage with caffeine tells me something is bothering you.''

She nodded and played with the juice can. ''Betty

Mayfield called today, just as I was leaving to go and visit Nonna.''

Betty Mayfield was the real-estate agent who handled the rental of Cara's town house.

"Are your tenants having a problem of some kind?''

"No, but they gave their notice. They're buying a house and want to move out at the end of the month.''

"I see.'' The food Neil had eaten seemed to be forming a mass in his stomach.

"I told Betty not to rent my town house out to other tenants. She made the assumption that I was considering putting it up for sale. I felt kind of dishonest because I didn't correct her.''

She wanted the town house vacant so that she could move back into it herself after Sophia passed away. That could happen any day, according to the prognosis.

"Cara, I want to take care of you. Of you and the baby. You can have the larger bedroom and bath.''

"You and I both need some breathing room we won't have living in the same house. I'm hoping you'll start sleeping again and get your appetite back once your life returns to normal.''

"I'm not concerned about *me*. I'll get by.''

"But *I* am concerned about you.'' She glanced down at her stomach, and her expression grew tender. "We won't be that far away. If I need you, I'll call, and you can be there in ten minutes.''

"You're not planning to file for a legal separation?"

"Not right away. Before I do anything like that, I'll discuss it with you."

It was some small consolation that she wasn't in a hurry to dissolve their marriage.

If Neil had been convinced in his heart that she and their child were better off living with him, he would have applied more pressure. But maybe he was selfishly thinking only of himself. Maybe Cara knew best.

The one thing Neil was certain of was that he couldn't protect them from harm twenty-four hours a day, whether they lived under his roof or not. That inability haunted him.

"I feel fine. In fact, I've never felt better." Cara continued to protest as Neil steered her toward the door, forcibly evicting her from the kitchen. "You cooked supper again tonight. I should clean up."

"It won't take me fifteen minutes."

"At least let me help."

"We'll just bump into each other."

The image his words raised sent a shiver of feminine pleasure through Cara. She wanted so badly to come back with a seductive remark like "Sounds nice to me" or "That's the whole idea." Being pregnant hadn't made her any less physically responsive to Neil. In fact, she seemed to have become more sensuous.

His hands felt so strong and gentle on her shoulders. So masculine. She longed for him to touch and caress every inch of her body. For all she knew, he might be turned off by the idea of sex with a pregnant woman. Although, the way he looked at her, taking note of her burgeoning figure, sure didn't translate as disgust. However tempted he might be to break their no-sex policy a third time, he exerted that iron self-control of his.

"Lie on the sofa and take it easy," he ordered her.

"Yes, master."

He smacked her lightly on the bottom and Cara grumbled, rubbing the spot, "Bully." But her voice gave away the fact that she was smiling. She loved being gently manhandled by him. Loved the way he coddled her.

Loved him. So much.

Cara hated to think of moving out of his house, not seeing him every morning when she awoke, not spending every evening with him. But what choice did she have? She couldn't foist her little girl or boy on him. Nor did she want her son or daughter to grow up in the same house with a reluctant daddy.

Neil had to commit himself voluntarily to being husband and father. Make the commitment because he *wanted* to make it. Not because he was trapped by circumstances.

Whatever the future held, Cara wasn't going to fret and worry in advance. She was taking one day at a time. Visiting her dying grandmother had reinforced the awareness that each day, each hour is precious.

After clicking on the TV and placing the remote on

the lamp table near Neil's recliner, Cara made herself comfortable on the sofa. He joined her within the fifteen minutes he'd allotted himself for the kitchen cleanup, and they watched a new game show that had become all the rage.

Cara stayed alert, enjoying the challenge of trying to come up with the correct answers herself while Neil played home contestant, too. After the game show had ended, Neil flipped to another channel. A dramatic series they both liked featuring a big-city police department came on. About midway through the program, Cara's eyelids grew heavy and kept dropping. During a commercial break, she said sleepily, "I should probably get up and go to bed...."

But the sofa was incredibly comfortable. Cara couldn't seem to get her body into motion. She stayed where she was and fell soundly asleep.

Neil's voice penetrated her consciousness. "Cara, time for bed, sweetheart." He was nearby, she could tell.

"S'okay," she mumbled. "After the news goes off."

"The news is over." He grasped her shoulder and shook her gently. "Come on. I'll help you to your bedroom."

He manually got her into a sitting position and then lifted her onto her feet. Before Cara could marshal her coordination, he apparently gave up on the notion of her walking because he picked her up in his arms.

"You'll hurt your back." Her drowsy voice held

too much pleasure in his strength to qualify as much of an objection. "I've gained ten pounds. Part of it in my chest and fanny."

"Hush. You're not too heavy."

He was carrying her easily toward the hallway to their bedrooms.

"Why do we women love this caveman stuff?"

"Probably for the same reason men like it."

"In my mind's eye, I can see your muscles rippling in your back and shoulders."

"Cara." His tone was only part reproof.

He maneuvered through the open door of her bedroom. Near the bed he stood her on her feet. Cara hugged him around the waist, and he hugged her back. "Thank you," she whispered.

"Can you manage?" he asked, his voice husky.

"Hold me a minute and then you can unzip my dress and undo my bra."

"Where's your nightgown?"

"Folded up. Under my pillow. Just like Nonna taught me."

All too soon he released her, slowly, as though making sure she wouldn't topple. "Let's get you into bed, sweetheart," he said.

Cara sighed. "That was such a short minute." She turned her back to him. The only light in the room came from the hallway, but it was sufficient for the purpose of undressing, donning her nightgown and climbing into bed.

If only he would climb in with her, hold her, touch her. A languid desire mixed with Cara's drowsiness.

Her dress loosened as Neil unzipped it. Then her bra went slack after he'd unfastened it. "Hmm. That's nice," she murmured and pulled her arms free of dress and bra. Both garments fell to the carpet, and Cara was naked except for her panties.

Neil was motionless behind her. "My nightgown. Under the pillow," she said. Her real request was one she shouldn't be making: Touch me, please. She felt his hot breath on her shoulder and then his lips. His hands settled at her waist. Cara took them and urged them forward and upward. He cupped her breasts, and the ecstatic sensations forced a moan of pleasure from her throat.

"You're twice as beautiful and sexy now," he said, kissing her neck and sending more shivers of delight through her.

"Twice as sexy? Really? I know I'm twice as attracted to you these days. And I didn't think that was possible."

"What are we going to do, Cara?"

He meant, How were they going to resolve their problems? Cara didn't want to discuss problems or conflicts tonight. She wanted Neil to take her to bed and make love to her. She wanted to sleep cuddled up to him. Rather than spell out her answer in words, she turned around and drew his head down to kiss him. She said everything that needed saying with her lips and tongue, including please.

He spoke back in kind with passion and tenderness, agreeing to a night of heaven that would only be a respite from reality.

And heaven it was. On those few other occasions they'd made love, Cara had experienced unendurable bliss during their foreplay, but tonight she seemed more sensitized to the pleasure of his caresses and erotic attentions to her body. Also to the pleasure that came from stroking and fondling him and rendering him momentarily helpless with male arousal.

Coupling their bodies had been an act of love before, and again it proved to be beautiful and emotional. The speedy climb to release took Cara to a higher pinnacle of sensation than seemed possible. Satisfaction couldn't have been sweeter, although she wished she could have savored it longer instead of falling almost instantly asleep.

At no point had she deluded herself into believing that their transcendent lovemaking would accomplish what it hadn't before and produce a magic formula for happiness. When she and Neil awoke the next day, she would still be pregnant with a child he hadn't wanted to father and was afraid to take into his affections. He would still be wracked with anxiety that harm would befall her.

Cara had simply put all that out of her mind.

"Telephone for you, Neil," said Peewee. "Your mother-in-law."

Here it was, the telephone call he'd been dreading,

Neil thought. Sophia had passed away. Even though Cara thought she was prepared for the inevitable, he knew she really wasn't. Heavy-hearted, he spoke into the receiver, "Hello, Miss Rose."

As a child he'd adopted the southernism of softening formality and addressing older people he knew well by their first names with the prefix Miss or Mr. Rose LaCroix had been Miss Rose to him all his life.

"I'm not calling with sad news, Neil. Not today," she hastened to tell him.

"Thank God."

"Mamma would like for you to come and see her, if you can get away from the store."

Surprise kept him from replying immediately. "Of course I can get away. Shall I come over now?"

"Would you?"

"Cara's not here at the moment." He wasn't sure whether he was supposed to come alone or bring Cara.

"Mamma wanted to talk to you privately."

"I'm on my way."

Neil could guess what Sophia would say to him. She would extract a promise from him that he would look after Cara. A promise he could give with utmost sincerity. Neil planned to see that Cara and their child never lacked for anything money could buy, and he would always be there for them, whatever happened.

At the LaCroix home, his mother-in-law took him to Sophia's bedroom and departed. Sophia's appearance didn't shock him. He'd visited her briefly with Cara several times during recent weeks. On those occasions, too, he'd marveled at her serenity. Her disease hadn't made inroads on her spirit or her faith. Not the first complaint had he ever heard her make along the lines of "Why me?"

"It was good of you to come, Neil," she said after he'd kissed her on the cheek and sat in the chair near her bed. "But you were always such a good boy. So kind and considerate. When I heard about the death of your wife and little boy, I was so sorry such a terrible thing had happened to you. I knew you would take it hard."

"I did take it hard, Miss Sophia. It's the kind of thing that can't be easy. You lost your husband at a relatively young age." She hadn't seemed young to him at the time, but she'd only been in her late forties when she came to live with Cara's parents, a widow.

"My Tony was fifty-two when he died. I thought God was cruel, but I discovered it's true that our Heavenly Father never takes a blessing away without showering more blessings as life goes on." She smiled a peaceful smile and fingered the rosary that she held in her hand as though she were counting off blessings that had enriched her long life.

"What if—" Neil broke off.

"What if He takes away those blessings, too? That could happen. It might not happen, too. Then what?" It wasn't a rhetorical question. She seemed to expect an answer.

"I guess we miss out on the good as well as the bad if we're afraid to accept blessings."

"Let yourself be happy. God will give you the strength you need during bad times. He did before, didn't He?"

Neil nodded. He hesitated, then asked, "Has Cara told you I'm not a happy person?"

"Oh, no. I see with my eyes."

How much had this wise old woman seen through? he wondered. Had she been playing a role at their wedding, too? If so, he needed to reassure her. "I love her with all my heart, Miss Sophia."

"Yes, you do."

Plainly she'd had no doubts on that score. Neil could see that she was tiring and needed to rest. "This talk has done me a world of good," he said, rising. More than his sessions with a therapist.

"My Cara will make you a good wife. You let her take care of you."

Neil gave her a parting kiss on the cheek. She'd already dozed off as he was leaving the bedroom. His eyes glazed with tears as he told her silently, "I sure wish you were going to be around a few more years, Miss Sophia. I'm going to miss you."

Instead of returning to the store, Neil drove to a park and got out and walked around. He felt the need for solitude. He wanted to mull over his conversation with Cara's grandmother. There were preschool children playing in a playground. Neil watched them and imagined himself in a couple of years here in this same park with his little daughter or son.

That option was one of Sophia's "blessings,"

which he could either embrace or shun. The same applied to turning his marriage into a real marriage, to becoming Cara's husband in the fullest sense.

Could he find the courage to accept the blessing of a new family that might be snatched away from him? Neil believed he could.

Could and would.

By now Cara would have returned to the store. Neil found himself suddenly eager to see her, to share his mental breakthrough. Everything would be different now, holding her in his arms, kissing her, making love to her, discussing the future. All of which he wanted to do right away.

Using his cell phone, Neil called the store. Allison answered the phone and said, "Cara's not back yet. She must have gotten sidetracked."

"Have her call me at my cell-phone number."

"Will do."

Neil was tempted to drive around town and search for Cara. Instead he drove straight home. Getting out of his pickup, he looked at the nondescript one-story brick house, at the minimal landscaping. He glanced at a spot on the lawn near the street and visualized the For Sale sign that would go up.

They would buy a lot and build a house. A family house with a fenced-in backyard. He had some ideas and he was sure Cara would have lots of input, too. It wouldn't be feasible to aim for moving into a custom-built home before the baby arrived, but maybe within two or three months afterwards. Not *the* baby, *our* baby, Neil corrected himself.

He went inside and stood in the middle of the living room, eyeing the furniture with a critical eye. All of this cast-off stuff he'd gotten from his parents' house could be carted off to a charity outlet. It had served his purpose, but Cara would want new furniture for their house.

She would want a garage that wasn't an automotive shop, too. No problem, Neil reflected. His hobby of restoring old cars had simply been a means of occupying time. He would be busy with other projects now, much more meaningful projects. In fact, he doubted he would even finish restoring the Corvette. He knew a guy who would jump at the chance to buy it.

Neil paced and formulated plans, cell phone in hand. He would have expected Cara to call him by now. Whatever she was doing, she would have her cell phone with her. She always checked in often and let Neil know her whereabouts. Let him know that she was safe.

"Finally," he said aloud as his cell phone came to life. A glance at the number on the tiny screen told him Cara must have gotten back to the store.

"Hi, where've you been?" he asked.

"Neil, it's me," Allison said. His blood turned to ice at her tone. Something was wrong, terribly wrong. "Cara was in a bad accident. Her car was totalled."

Neil couldn't hear the rest of what she said. A roaring in his ears drowned her out.

Chapter Fifteen

"Sir! Stop!"

"My wife was brought here in an ambulance. I have to see her."

"What's your wife's name?"

"Cara Griffin."

"A doctor is with her. You'll have to wait in the visitors' lounge."

"Dammit, I'm not waiting anywhere! I have to see my wife!"

"Sir, I'll get Security."

Lying in a cubicle in the hospital Emergency ward, Cara had heard the heated conversation and barely recognized Neil's frantic voice. He was shouting at the woman carrying on the exchange with him, clearly a hospital employee.

"Please," Cara begged the physician examining her. "Bring my husband in. He needs to make sure I'm alive. He lost his first wife and child in a tragic car accident."

The doctor left her and intervened. "Follow me, Mr. Griffin," he said. "Your wife was very lucky. She sustained no serious injuries, just a few bruises."

"And our baby?"

"There're no symptoms of miscarriage. We'll want to keep a close watch, do some tests."

"Thank God."

Though Neil had been following behind the physician, as instructed, he managed to be first into the cubicle. His haggard appearance made Cara want to cry. Instead she smiled and said, "I think I'll need a new car." He came over to the bed, walking as though his knees had gone weak with the same overwhelming relief written on his face.

Cara held out her arms, and he bent over and laid his cheek against hers. She hugged him and whispered, "I'm sorry I gave you such a scare."

The doctor spoke up. "If you will, Mr. Griffin, you can step outside and sit in the visitors' lounge while I complete my examination."

Neil complied without any argument.

After he'd gone, Cara's eyes filled with tears. The doctor gave her a sympathetic pat on the arm and handed her a couple of tissues. She wept quietly while he proceeded. No doubt he thought her emotionalism was an aftereffect of the trauma of her accident.

It was the trauma that Neil had experienced that caused her such despair. Her brush with death would have reinforced all his fears about risking tragedy again.

"You can go in and visit your wife now, Mr. Griffin."

"Thank you, Doctor." Neil had jumped up out of his chair at the appearance of the balding physician, who gave a clinical, but reassuring report that mother and baby both seemed fine.

"She put up a brave front until you came," the man said. "Then her emotions got the best of her, quite understandably."

Exactly what that meant, Neil wasn't sure, but he didn't stick around to ask questions. He would find out for himself.

One look at Cara's face told him she'd been crying. "Hi," she greeted him, mustering a brave smile.

Neil went over to the bed and kissed her tearstained cheeks, kissed her tenderly on the mouth. "Did you get the shakes, darling?"

She was gazing at him uncertainly. "You seem okay," she said.

"I am okay, now. I've settled down." He sat on the edge of the bed and picked up her hands and held them. "Your mother is on the way. And goodness knows how many of your sisters and brothers and sisters-in-law and brothers-in-law will be showing up.

I've had nonstop conversations on my cell phone out in the waiting room."

"You even seem...*more* okay."

He squeezed her hands and teased, "'More okay?' Your high-school English teacher might frown over that usage."

"Mrs. Dunlop frowned over most of my usages."

Neil chuckled, and she smiled at him, a genuine smile, her buoyant spirit reviving. "I went to visit your grandmother today."

"You did?"

He nodded. "She had your mother call and ask me to come. You know what? I'm not sure we pulled the wool over her eyes."

"Nonna has never seemed suspicious to me."

"She's a wise lady. We had a talk that helped me get my head on straight. After I left your parents' house, I went to the park and watched some little kids play for a while." He bent and kissed the gentle swell of her stomach.

She caressed his head. "Did you feel sad watching them play?"

"No, I wasn't sad. There was too much to be glad about."

A second passed while she absorbed his words. "What did you do next?"

"I called the store to ask you to meet me at our house. I went there and waited for you to phone me on my cell phone. Instead Allison called."

"With the news I'd had an accident." Cara gazed at him anxiously.

"I freaked out for about half a minute and didn't even get all the details. Drove here like a maniac. You know the rest." He kissed her and she wrapped her arms around his neck keeping his face close to hers.

"You said Nonna helped you get your head on straight," she said. "Just how straight is 'straight'?"

"Straight enough to decide I want to sell my house and build us another house."

"Really?" She sounded and looked delighted. "What fun."

"Straight enough to know there's no way I'll let you move into your town house or anywhere else without me."

"You seem definite about that."

"Very definite."

She kissed him and waited expectantly for him to say more. Neil knew what she wanted to hear. And what he could finally tell her with absolute sincerity. "I'm excited about our baby, Cara."

"Oh, Neil, that makes me so happy!"

"Sweetheart, don't cry," he pleaded as two huge tears rolled down her cheeks. Tenderly he wiped them away.

"They're happy tears. Relieved tears. You have no idea how scared I was that my car wreck had killed any chance of our staying together."

"Your car wreck brought home the wisdom of Sophia's philosophy of living every day to the fullest and accepting our blessings. I regret these months I've wasted, I regret our honeymoon.''

"I don't,'' she declared. "There were precious moments mixed in.''

They kissed, and she whispered happily, "I love you.''

"I love you.'' Neil gazed into her eyes, savoring this instant in time. He felt a deep sense of peace along with his joy and anticipation. Yesterday was past and tomorrow was ahead, a tomorrow he looked forward to. What was really important, though, was *now*.

* * * * *

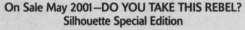
 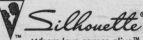

Silhouette® —
where love comes alive—online...

eHARLEQUIN.com

your romantic books

♥ **Shop online!** Visit Shop eHarlequin and discover a wide selection of new releases and classic favorites at great discounted prices.

♥ **Read** our daily and weekly Internet exclusive serials, and participate in our interactive novel in the reading room.

♥ **Ever dreamed of being a writer?** Enter your chapter for a chance to become a featured author in our Writing Round Robin novel.

your romantic life

♥ **Check out** our feature articles on dating, flirting and other important romance topics and get your daily love dose with tips on how to keep the romance alive every day.

your community

♥ **Have a Heart-to-Heart** with other members about the latest books and meet your favorite authors.

♥ **Discuss** your romantic dilemma in the Tales from the Heart message board.

your romantic escapes

♥ **Learn** what the stars have in store for you with our daily Passionscopes and weekly Erotiscopes.

♥ **Get** the latest scoop on your favorite royals in Royal Romance.

SINTA1R

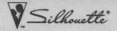
Silhouette®

SPECIAL EDITION™

is delighted to present

The
Stockwells
of Texas

Available January—May 2001

**Where family secrets, scandalous pasts
and unexpected love wreak havoc on the lives
of the infamous Stockwells of Texas!**

THE TYCOON'S INSTANT DAUGHTER
by Christine Rimmer
(SE #1369) on sale January 2001

SEVEN MONTHS AND COUNTING...
by Myrna Temte
(SE #1375) on sale February 2001

HER UNFORGETTABLE FIANCÉ
by Allison Leigh
(SE #1381) on sale March 2001

THE MILLIONAIRE AND THE MOM
by Patricia Kay
(SE #1387) on sale April 2001

THE CATTLEMAN AND THE VIRGIN HEIRESS
by Jackie Merritt
(SE #1393) on sale May 2001

Available at your favorite retail outlet.

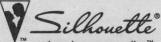

Silhouette®
Where love comes alive™

Visit Silhouette at www.eHarlequin.com   SSESOT